ELLA

Stephen Moran

Visit the Website to follow the story at
http://www.stephenjohnmoran.com/

For information contact StephenJohnMoran@gmail.com

Published by Moran Publishing
11173 African Sunset Street
Henderson, NV 89052

To my beautiful wife, Maggie. There are no words—thank you for marrying me. You are my inspiration and my happiness. Your help at every stage of this process pushed the book over the finish line. Truly, this couldn't have happened without you. To many more years of happiness.

ACKNOWLEDGEMENTS

The Editor – Su A. Joo – You helped me bring Ella from a tattered draft to a readable manuscript. Your insight was and is invaluable and I look forward to working with you on future projects. All I can say is Thank you!!! Writers looking for editing services, check out her website – http://sirraedits.com

To the cover artist – Marielle van Broekhoven – Your painting of Ella truly inspired me to reach new levels. You captured her spirit and her being in a way that made it possible for me to deepen my understanding of her character and story. No thanks can cover it—however, I say thank you!!!! Check out her wonderful paintings at http://www.mariellevanbroekhoven.com

I'd like to thank Toni Rakestraw and her daughter Morwenna for working with me on the cover and interior design for this book. Thank you for answering the countless e-mails and walking me through this process!

To Justin Bogdanovitch, thank you for being a constant friend throughout this process. You're always there to answer questions and give timely pep talks that keep me going. I couldn't have done it without you!!!

To Monica Mills, I can't thank you enough for always being there to read the latest installments and to offer support and constant feedback, which is so very essential to a writer. I hope soon to see a book of yours in print, too!

TABLE OF CONTENTS

UXBRIDGE, MA

A man waits in line for coffee as I attempt to finish writing a chapter before my break ends. He taps expensive leather shoes against the filthy floor, which is covered with winter mess despite constant mopping. Coffee orders tend to increase on cold, snowy days in January and the line is long at this hour. Staring at a young brunette struggling to keep up, who is only doing her job, he grunts and crosses his arms in her direction.

I see a vein pulsing in his neck and feel an overwhelming desire to drive one of the icicle spikes hanging from the door into his skin. Placing the pen on my notebook, I rise and make my way behind the counter to help my co-worker.

"Can I help you?" Tying the apron, I wait for him to speak. *I won't let him ruin her day when he is here to see me.*

While his eyes travel over my body, a crooked smile rises on his face. Leaning close to the counter, he whispers in my direction. "I'm surprised you came off break to help me. I don't suppose you'll come over to my place later for drinks."

Gripping the blender handle with my fingers, I count to ten in my head to let a pulse of anger subside. *I will not give in to his taunts.* "Same story every day. Isn't it illegal to offer drinks to a minor?"

1

"I can keep a secret if you can."

"Why can't you stop asking me? It's been months of this."

"It's your last day. How can one little drink hurt?"

That part is true. It's my last day.

As I make his coffee, thoughts of my upcoming journey flood my mind. There isn't a real plan, not even a destination. Simply, I know that I must leave Uxbridge. I'm never going to make a difference or be anyone in this town. The biggest question remains. How far will my car make it? Can I reach NYC?

"You're too old for me." I hand the cup over the counter.

He rubs a finger along my palm, which makes me shiver. It's always the same harassment I encounter every day with men like him.

"Why did you quit?" Without replying to my statement, he still tries to massage my hand.

I yank it away from him. "You know. I can't finish my novel in this place. I'm hitting the road in search of adventure."

Did anyone notice I slipped and said *you know*? Why do I continue the charade of pretending when everyone knows? It's a small town, there are no secrets.

"Don't waste your time with writing. There's no money in it. Besides, nobody reads anymore."

I bite my lower lip. "I've told you a dozen times, I *am* a writer. I couldn't give up writing any more than you could stop sexually harassing young girls."

Co-workers and customers nearby start to laugh. The man takes a sip of his coffee, probably trying to gather courage or words for his next assault.

"Avoiding me will only delay the inevitable and makes you look guilty." He slides his business card toward me on the counter. Turning away before I can react, he exits with his coffee.

Ugh, pervert.

Slipping the card into my pocket, I remove the apron and return to writing. I hear people talking about me, but I won't give them the pleasure of showing emotion. *Ignore the distraction and get back to work.*

I hold the pen as my mind searches for words, but the only word repeating in my mind like a broken record is...Ray.

No, I don't want to get into it now. I haven't decided what to do about him. It's been months, and he didn't respond to my plea for help when I sent him what little I wrote of my novel. What good is a writing mentor if he won't read your book? Though, to be fair, Ray is a lot more than a mentor. He is...

A finger taps my shoulder, startling me. It's my manager, who is looking down at me over his horn-rimmed eyeglasses. He hands me an envelope along with an awkward sort of hug, failing to pull me completely into his arms.

"We'll miss you around here." Then he goes on and on.

He lets me go without finishing my shift, which is weird. *Who cares?* I'm out of here.

The frigid cold nips my face, forcing me to make a run for my car over the black ice. I slip and fight to maintain balance, my fingers gripping the handle and yanking the door open. Blowing into my hands for warmth, I try to start the car. Nothing. Is it my battery, my starter, or something else? This is what I get for driving a *Ford*. I sigh.

I make another attempt, but the engine won't turn. Looking around I see the cop from earlier sitting in a Ford across the parking lot, watching me. After several more attempts, I jump out and slam the door, which sends ice chards flying from my car. The cop flicks his high beams at me, cutting a swath of light in the descending darkness of early evening.

There being no other options, I decide to walk across the parking lot toward his Crown Victoria.

He pretends to look in every direction other than mine and he flinches and spills coffee on his slacks when I open the door.

"Damn it, Ella. Don't just open the door and get in. People are *always* watching."

I ignore him. "Do you have the file?"

He nods. "This could get me fired. I hope you know that."

While his whining continues, I glare at him. Blah, blah, blah... It doesn't matter what else happens as long as I get the file. It's the *only* reason I've tolerated his presence.

Cursing, he pulls onto the road without looking, causing the tires to slide in the slushy dirt. My hand reaches for the radio to find a song I like, music that I'm quite certain he hates. Singing along, I ignore his noticeable annoyance until he parks in my driveway.

"I doubt we're a secret in this town," I say.

I hop out of the car and walk inside. There's no need to turn around to know he will follow. The engine goes silent. His boots squish and squeak in the snow, coming closer until I feel him press against my back.

"Just open the door. It doesn't matter anymore," he grumbles.

Inside, I walk to the bedroom to change, not bothering to close the door. The wet winter clothes peel off my body. Putting on sweat pants, I enter the living room. His eyes lock onto my bare flesh and a smile changes to a frown as I pull a t-shirt over my head.

"Are you staying for dinner again?"

I know what the answer will be, so I grab the pots and pans for pasta and meatballs. Men will eat anything as long as they don't have to cook. I notice him arranging my books in alphabetical order. Sighing, I turn my attention back to cooking.

"You look very pretty."

I turn my head and stick my tongue out at him. "I'm wearing sweatpants, wise guy."

"You're barefoot and cooking me dinner." He winks.

Men. "Forget that. You still haven't told me what you think of my novel. You read it, right?"

"I read a few pages but couldn't go on. How can I read a book that doesn't have a title?"

"I don't need a title yet. It's a work in progress."

"Make the title reflect the story." He walks over and leans against the counter, watching me stir the pasta. "In other words, what's this novel about?"

"The rise of women."

Chuckling, he opens a bottle of wine and avoids looking at me. "Nobody wants to read about that. People want to escape reality."

"What should I write about, fucking vampires that sparkle?" I accentuate each word by slamming the spatula on the end of the skillet.

"I don't know. Sex and violence usually do the trick. That's all I can say. After all, I'm a cop, not a writer."

"That, I know."

Despite my anger, I put an extra helping of meatballs on his plate. We sit and begin to eat, watching each other and drinking wine. He finishes and I get up to make him another plate when he breaks the silence.

"I must ask you one more question about that night."

I slam my palm on the table, spilling wine on the tablecloth. Neither of us moves, and for a span of minutes, the ticking of my wall clock serves as the only sound in the room. I'm not going to talk about this with him. No. Not again.

"Why can't you let this go? It's been six months. You have asked me the same questions a hundred different ways. Why must you obsess over it?"

"Because a man died!"

"A man that three witnesses testified to seeing assault and rape me..."

He cuts me off. "Yes, but..."

I cut him off, too. "Roger, there are no ifs or buts. A man assaulted me. I killed him. The end."

"There are...inconsistencies in your statements," he says, measuring his words.

"I spent five years locked in a nut house, and you're surprised there are *inconsistencies* in my statement? And they say I'm crazy." My body trembles and my heart races.

6

He laughs, but his eyes probe me with unsaid questions and commentary. He pours another glass of wine, returning to his plate of pasta. His chewing slows and I feel his eyes on me. I can almost detect the sparks inside his mind—ideas churning in that cop orb that won't let me out. My hand grips the bread knife, and the powerful urge to ram it into his neck comes over me.

"The part I don't understand..." He stops to finish chewing.

I'm freaking out as I wait for doom, but I just listen.

"Where did all the money go?"

Money? What money is he talking about? He knows I have no money. Gulping the wine, I watch him for any clue. "What?" The word cracks in my throat.

"And why do you have men following you?"

"You should be able to answer that better than I can," I murmur, sliding the knife off the table and into my lap. Can I reach him before he can react?

"One man seems to be a professional, though not a cop. The other one is..."

I try to speak, but my voice fails me.

"The FBI." A wide smile rises on his fat cheeks.

"I haven't noticed anyone following me." I try to slow my breathing, the pace of my heart clouding my thoughts.

"You'd be the last to know."

I wince. This cop logic seems sound, but what does he really know? What does he want me to say? After gathering my courage, I blurt out the only thing on my mind. "Tell me about the money."

He taps his fingers on the table in drumroll imitation as I squirm in my seat, ready to leap at him. My phone vibrates with a new text message from an unknown number. As I grab the phone, Roger puts down his fork.

"Millions left to you have gone missing." He shoots a sharp glance toward me.

"What? I don't have millions of anything, let alone dollars." I shake my head.

When I try to read the message on my phone, Roger's eyes follow.

"All accounts are dated on the day of your eighteenth birthday."

This can't be true. Am I rich? But Roger has nothing to gain from lying. Why would he make this up?

"Tell me what's in the FBI file."

A wide grin spreads over his face when he opens the file. He appears proud to have this power over me.

"It says here. 5' 5", eyes pale blue, hair blonde, skin like porcelain. Very attractive, could be a model, and uses her sexual attraction as a weapon. Quite intelligent. Prone to lying and manipulation to achieve goals. No moral or societal boundaries apply in her mind. Abused by father for years, guilty of patricide. Molested by the—"

Bolting out of my seat, I grab his arm and put my hand over his mouth. I clench my teeth. "Do. Not. Finish. That. Sentence." *If you do, it will be your last mistake.*

Although he appears shocked, he remains still.

Shaking my head, I take my hand off of his mouth and finally read the text message on my phone.

Get out of the house. Do not tell him anything. Walk to the end of your street. Run through the woods to lose him. There will be a blue '74 Firebird waiting in the abandoned parking lot next to the car dealership. Keys are in the ignition. Drive to 555 Holden Avenue in Newtown, Connecticut.

I fall back into my seat and freeze. There are people watching. I feel my face flush, but before I can let the information settle in my head, the phone buzzes with another text.

DO NOT KILL HIM. HE IS WIRED. GET OUT NOW!

I slam the chair back against the refrigerator and bolt up. Walking straight to the entryway, I throw on wool socks, boots, and a winter jacket. His expression switches from shock to curiosity. I suppose this isn't how he thought I'd react to his secrets.

Ignoring the advice of the text, I take the time to pack my writing materials, a computer tablet, and an extra phone charger. Roger continues drinking at the table. Maybe he doesn't notice or care that I'm getting ready to leave. Pulling a knit cap over my hair, I exit the apartment without a word.

The cold assaults me again the instant I step outside. Expecting him to follow me on foot or by car, I hurry down the road, but my footsteps are the only sound I hear. When I reach the woods and look back, he's just leaving my apartment. I sprint through the woods. The wind forces tears down my cheeks. I near the clearing and see the Firebird next to a streetlamp, just as the text said. What a relief.

The door isn't locked. I jump inside and turn the key that's in the ignition. I smile at the loud roar. A glint of light catches my attention and I realize that there's a pistol on the passenger's seat. My smile lingers as I drive toward the highway. At this rate, I will arrive at the address in less than two hours.

Excitement fills me. I'm on an adventure. No more boring coffee shop. No more of this small town of hicks. I reach for the radio, but my phone buzzes again.

See you soon.

HOLDEN FARMS

The countryside hits like an echo within my memory—lazy avenues, patient pedestrians, and only one stop light in town. Having visited just the one time on the 4th of July long ago prevents me from recognizing anything particular. The GPS navigation leads me toward the high hills on the far side of town beyond the endless horse stables and the snow covered hills dotted with corn stalks.

When I reach an avenue lined by oak firs, the GPS announces that I'm at the destination. A sprawling mansion comes into view—the front entrance of arched columns leads to castle towers wide enough for several guards. Black gates twice my height bar the way, which are in complete disrepair, the crooked metal covered by layers of moss and dust.

Pushing aside my fear, I approach the gates, huddling my shoulders against a brisk wind. Shoving the handle makes it rattle, but it doesn't budge. This time, I push with my shoulder and shake the gate with force. Still, nothing. I gaze at the mansion for a few minutes, hoping for any sign of life. The wind is the only company I find.

Snapping myself out of my brief reverie, I pop open the trunk and grab the tire iron. I search for a weak spot to apply leverage. The sound of tires crunching the snow startles me. It's very close. Dropping the iron, I turn and walk toward the sound. At the same time, a police car bathes the area in a sea of red, white, and blue. Strangely, there's no siren to match the lights, but a cop steps out into the night.

"Put your hands in the air. Slowly."

Just. Fucking. Perfect.

Inching my arms up to the night sky, I follow his command.

"What are you doing at that gate? You trying to break in?" He gestures with his head at the spot where I left the iron.

"I'm meeting someone." There's no reason to lie.

"This is private property and you're trespassing." He takes a step in my direction. Tall, tanned, and handsome in a clean, brown uniform, he studies me for a moment.

I remain still, waiting for him to get closer. I see his pale blue eyes, nearly the same color as my own.

"Do you know the owners of this property?"

"Everyone knows this mansion belongs to the Holdens." I point at the broken sign hanging by one of the two metal spokes that once held it to the gate.

"It's too cold for jokes. Do you want me to take you in? What's your name?"

"Ella Thomas." My voice shake along with my body. "Can I at least put my hands down? I'm freezing."

"Go ahead." He speaks into a radio handset on his shoulder. After repeating my name to the dispatcher, he waits. When there is no immediate response, he resumes his questioning. "Who are you here to see again?"

I wrap my arms around me. "I know Ray Holden."

Narrowing his eyes, he turns his attention to the sound of a voice coming from the headset. His eyes widens, and his mouth drops open. "Ray Holden died almost five years ago."

"What?" It *can't* be true. No, it's *not* true.

"He died in a terrorist attack in NYC. How don't you know that?"

I was locked away in a nut house. "You must be mistaken."

"It was big news in this town. Almost as big as when Ray's father died, and the fortune was contested in court."

Crossing my arms tighter, I breathe deeply, letting the cold air fill my lungs. *He can't do anything to me.* "What did the dispatcher tell you? Your face lost a little color there, I swear it."

"She informed me that this property belongs to you."

My feet are frozen to the ground. I can feel my pulse pound the back of my eyes, throbbing with my internal disbelief. "You can't be serious."

The flashing lights are giving me a headache as I wait for him to speak. He opens his mouth several times, but no words follow. Or nothing is registering in my brain. Backing away from me, he gets into his car and reverses course down the avenue. The flashing lights turn off as the car disappears from my view.

Without thinking, I retrieve the iron and begin swinging at the gate. It doesn't take long for me to manage to create a wedge wide enough to squeeze my body through it. I run over the pea gravel driveway to the main entrance, eager to get out of the cold. The fear creeps up again when the door opens just as I approach. The foyer seems empty and as neglected as the outside entrance, filled with cobwebs and shadows.

"Hello?"

Nothing. Someone must be here. Who opened the door? I step into the mansion, which is a sea of white sheets covering all the furnishings. The wood of the main spiral staircase is covered in thick layers of dust and grime. The cop may have been telling the truth. Nobody lives here. Shroud covered paintings line the creaky, winding stairs. The home itself seems to take notice of my presence. Through a door to the left, I see a library, so I walk inside. The room is dominated by a massive desk in front of a fireplace.

On the desk, there's a solitary book—not a lamp, a pen, or even a sheet of paper—just one book. I pick it up. It appears to be a journal of some sort. The cover is baby blue with purple edging, and a gold-embossed cord wound around it, keeping it closed. Unwinding the cord, I open the journal. The first page begins with a surprise.

Dedicated to Ella Thomas,
With love

My trembling hand turns a page and reveals a title.

Preface to a Suicide
by
Ray Holden.

The next page is filled with tightly handwritten lines that are too small to read. I pull the book closer and read the first line.

It is purely out of concern for my family's well-being that I have decided to write in this journal.

As I repeat the sentence in my mind to make sense of the words, I hear the door close behind me. I spin around to see an old man clad in a black tuxedo staring at me with arms tucked behind his back and a smile on his face.

"Hello, Ella. Welcome home."

HELLO, GEORGE

"Who are you?"

"You may call me Mr. Johnson," the man says.

"Is Ray dead, Mr. Johnson?"

"According to the coroner in NYC, yes," he says with a calm demeanor.

What a curious thing to say... Picking at my cuticles, I start to study him. The whites and grays of his receding hairline is an indication of his old age, but his severe jaw seems undaunted by age. I watch him glide across the room to a particular bookcase. When he touches a hidden mechanism, the middle shelf spins to reveal a row of bottles.

"You are an exquisite beauty, of that there can be no doubt. And I'm not usually one to say such things. However, seeing as we've just become acquainted, my word can't count for much." His voice is soothing, and his eyes scan me in a polite, courteous fashion. "What's your pleasure?"

Did he use the word exquisite in a sentence? "Whiskey. No ice," I mutter, trying not to laugh.

Taking a glass from a rack, he pours a generous amount from a bottle without a label. He spins it in front of me on the desk and ends his presentation with a half-bow.

"Whiskey. *Neat.*"

16

Not bothering to retort, I taste the whiskey. The hint of vanilla feels pleasant and warm.

"This is good stuff. What is it?"

"That bottle came from a distillery on Holden Farms."

Get out. This place feels more like a castle than a farm. On the walls, between paintings and sculptures, various firearms and killing instruments hang. I see an axe, a spear, a bow, a hammer, and a sword before he interrupts my train of thought.

"Can I ask you a question, Miss Thomas?"

I nod.

"You were followed here. Tell me what they want with you. Just tell me the truth because I already know almost everything."

Dragging my foot on the ground, I avoid his eyes. I blink while chopping and editing my response many times in my head. "I killed a boy at a party in self-defense. After the investigation, the police dropped the charges. I really don't know why they're still interested in me."

"I see." He adds, "You won't be able to avoid them by staying here. The FBI will simply get a court order."

"I know."

His eyes glint. "Are you telling me everything?"

"No." I brave a smile.

"Very well. Shall I show you to your apartment?"

He didn't even bat an eyelash when I told him I lied.

There are so many questions to ask, but fatigue proves stronger than curiosity. I don't know if this man is friend or foe...or something else entirely. In the end, he didn't give me a straight answer to any of my questions, and somehow, I get the impression that he never will.

"I want to look at the books, but I'm too tired, sir." *I am sick of calling men 'sir' and dream...*

He interrupts, reading my expression. "You don't want to read the books in this library without talking to me first. Please do not disregard this warning."

"Yes, grandpa." Shrugging, I grab a book just as he looks away. I see the title page. *Stories of Death by James Smith.* I hide it under the other and follow him out.

He leads me up the staircase to a second story apartment that consists of a bedroom, dressing room, and expansive bathroom. Furnished with only a bed, end table, mirror, and writing desk, it's a modest place, to say the least, compared to the luxury of the library. The dressing room is empty except for a safe on the floor.

"You can put whatever personal possessions you have in this room."

"Do you have the combination to the safe?"

"It's open, I believe."

Spinning the lock, I pull the handle to lift the top. That door springs open. *Jackpot.* I turn to look back at Mr. Johnson to see his reaction, but he's already gone. Letting out a big breath, I go through the contents of the safe: bundles of cash, several envelopes of various sizes, and a map with dots over different locations. The first envelope contains a list of financial accounts. Scanning the paper, I find names of big companies, U.S. Treasuries, and real estate holdings.

18

"Where's all the money going?" I frown, pointing at a graph that depicts a steady decline of value since inception on my 18th birthday.

"You wouldn't understand the answer." His reply is short and sharp. He seems to possess the ability to appear out of thin air.

I don't know what to think of his somewhat condescending reply. Returning my attention to the file, I go over the list of assets again. *This is all...mine?* The first thing I do is count the money. My mouth drops as I realize that I'm holding more than fifty thousand dollars in cold, hard cash. My heart thumps and I do not know what to say. I place the bills on the floor and move on to the second envelope with my name hand-written on the front. Sliding my finger under the flap, I rip it open and pull out a letter.

Ella,

You have come home, or you would not be reading this letter. I know how many questions you must have and assure you everything will be answered in good time. First, know that I am most definitely alive. No matter what you are told, rumors of my death...are inaccurate.

Holden Farms belong to you. Besides the property, you will be provided an income that is enough for you to live comfortably for the rest of your days. Mr. Johnson and the rest of the staff are there to serve you in any manner you desire.

Finally, the promise I made you on the day your father died can be fulfilled if it is still your wish. Mr. Johnson can give you the details when you are ready.

I hope to see you again,

Yours
Ray Holden

"Mr. Johnson?" I yell.

"Yes, Ella?" Again, he appears in the doorway as if conjured.

"Where is he?"

"I can't tell you. You're not ready."

What?

I hand over the letter to him, hoping that will give me more authority. He reads it for a few seconds before handing it back to me.

"Just as it is written."

What a jerk!

The heat begins to build up inside me while he stands tight-lipped. I can't read this man, and something tells me that he has no intention to confess. My gaze falls on the map. I pick it up and spread it over the top of the safe. The dots mark major cities, starting from Holden Farms and ending in Las Vegas.

"Vegas," I whisper.

"Don't even think about it. You don't have any idea what's going on. And for the second time, you are *not* ready."

"What's going on in Las Vegas?"

Again, no answer. Instead, he stares at me while I trace the line drawn through NYC, Cleveland, Chicago, and St. Louis. *He drove? Why?*

"Tell me what I need to do to be *ready*."

"You are simply too young. You haven't finished writing your novel, haven't been in a real relationship, and being a barista at a coffee shop was the only job you've had so far. Point blank. You're just a kid."

I clench my fists. *A kid that will jab a blade in your neck if you don't watch your attitude.* I take a deep breath to control my anger. I won't let him get to me. That will just prove his point.

"So, if I finish my novel and fuck a bunch of strangers, you'll tell me?" I yell, grabbing a bundle of cash. "Because I certainly don't need a job anymore."

Clucking his tongue, he shakes a finger at me. "Don't be vulgar. I just meant that you haven't lived. You aren't even old enough to drink."

"Imagine that story. Fucking my way across country in search of a long lost love."

"Ernest Hemingway said, in order to write about life, first you must live it." *That smile appears on his face again.*

"Wait. What's to stop me from driving out to Vegas?"

"I can't tell you that, either. But if you test me, you will find out. Please don't go there before your twenty-first birthday. You can't take full control of the assets left to you in the will until such time in any event."

A will? I'm puzzled at this point. Lost.

"What happens when I turn twenty-one?"

Without a pause, he answers, "At that time, I will determine if you are capable of handling the trust. If not, we will convene in Vegas again on your twenty-fifth birthday to repeat the process."

I shake my head. "Hold on. What happens with my money while it's in the trust or whatever?"

"A shell company controls it through various interests in Las Vegas." He crosses his arms behind him.

"Um...okay. So, basically, the money can be all gone or double or triple by the time I get control of the estate. Anything can happen, right?"

Unbelievable! Did Ray leave this money for me, or is he using me to hold it until he's ready to claim it? While I try to control my thoughts a machine beeps nearby, jolting me.

Mr. Johnson presses a button near the safe. The wall panels slide open and reveal a bank of television monitors—each displaying views from numerous security cameras on the property. The camera for the main gate beeps and flashes red. A Hispanic man with dark, slicked hair and wearing a black leather jacket is peering into the camera lens.

"Who's that?"

"The FBI," he says, eyes glued to the screen.

"Are you sure?"

"Positive."

Whoa. I guess he knows what he's talking about. I watch the man walking over the tire tracks left by my car and the police car. After a few minutes, he heads down the avenue and out of the camera's range.

"What does he want?" My brows pull together.

Mr. Johnson presses the button one more time, causing the monitors to go black and the wall to close. Pulling out a bottle from his pocket, he takes a pill out and places it on my hand. He walks into the bedroom and returns with a glass of water.

"Take it," he says.

I do as he requests. Whatever the pill is, it won't take long to take effect because I can barely keep my eyes open.

"One more thing, Mr. Johnson. What is your name?"

Before he can answer, I stumble into the bedroom and climb onto the bed. I'm barely conscious, but know he is right behind me. Without asking, he pulls down the bedding to let me slide my legs inside. He lifts the covers up to my chin and shuts off the light.

"George."

THE OPENING BELL

A horserace crashes into my dream and wakes me. My head is pounding and my mouth is dry. I hear bells ringing, which seems to be echoing from some lower chamber. Dragging myself out of bed, I slip on the white silk robe hanging on the door before following the noise. The sound ceases as I enter the great room downstairs. George is watching a giant TV that is built into the far wall.

"What's with the racket?" I say in a weak, raspy voice. A fog hovers over my mind, and I struggle to concentrate.

"Did the opening bell wake you?" He walks over to me with a tray that has a pitcher of juice, toast, and a newspaper on it.

"What time is it?" I blink and look around the room.

"The bell just rang, so it's nine-thirty in the morning."

There's some correlation between the bell and the time? I scratch my head. "Okay...I should still be sleeping," I mumble as I take a seat.

On the massive screen, random numbers float along the bottom in an incessant crawl. On the left of the screen, a talking head person spouts forth on European debt concerns. This makes no sense and makes me want to go back to bed. But the sight of the toast makes my stomach grumble in hunger.

"I'm starving. I mean...no bacon, sausage, pancakes, or even eggs?"

"Right away." Placing the tray on a table, he makes a quick exit.

"Don't forget the whiskey." *Nothing better than alcohol for breakfast.*

I don't know if he heard me, but it was worth a shot anyway. The throbbing pain in my brain forces me to sit and close my eyes. White streaks of bright pain flash inside my eyelids as the voice from the television interviews some very rich man on some very serious subject. The horses return to bellow at me and ring the bells again and again.

George taps my shoulder, waking me. The smell the bacon hits my nose before I open my eyes, and I can't help smiling. When I see the tumbler of whiskey, I look up at him and give him an approving nod. For now, I can say that he's a friend. I smother the pancakes with thick slabs of butter and syrup and let them sit. While I munch on the pieces of bacon, the pancakes soak up the butter and syrup. Just the way I like it.

"Change the channel. Please." *I want to eat, not fall back asleep.*

"You should watch this. Learn how to manage your money." He stares into my eyes.

"Learn by watching TV?" I snort.

"It's a start. If you're serious about women's issues for example, know that nothing can help the position of women more than financial education," he says before leaving the room.

No need to lecture me. I highly doubt that watching a TV show will give me the proper "financial education" when others go to school for years to get it. But I'll indulge him. Lifting my gaze to the screen, I listen to a man giving advice about buying gold. To wear? I don't understand much of what he says or the questions being asked of him. Terms fly at me: P/E ratio, EBITDA, dividends. After a few minutes, my pounding head is about to explode.

"God, George! This makes my headache worse!"

I don't mean to be an ungrateful bitch, but financial news at this time of the day seems excessive. Have respect for hangovers. Thank you. *Geez...*

When he comes back, he drops several pills into my hand and a glass of water on my tray. I'd ask, but at this moment, I don't care. After watching me take the pills, he motions for me to rest my head on the couch. Then he gently places a cool, wet towel on my forehead. His thoughtfulness seems a bit overboard, but I can't deny that it feels good. The words and the pain recede as I see a money machine that's riffing through bales of cash and spitting them into a giant, empty swimming pool.

"What are you doing with the money, Mister?" I ask the pool man.

He keeps feeding the bundles into the machine without looking at me. "It's your money."

A stiff wind lifts some of them high into the air, spiraling above my head like flies. I try to grab the bills, but they turn into sand and fall between my fingers.

26

"You have to earn it."

"How?" I yell, but no sound can be heard. Panic spreads down to my legs.

"Ella?"

The TV drones on with a woman's voice, asking me if I know where my money is. I want to tell her it's in the pool, but instead, I open my eyes. George is standing in front of me, tugging on tuxedo lapels with his thick fingers.

Rubbing my eyes, I pull my head up. "What was that? The pills you gave me."

"Something to help you relax." He taps his shoulders as if he were dusting.

"It did more than that..." I try to finish, but the lady begins a segment about women in business. It intrigues me.

"What would you say to all the women out there who are afraid to start businesses or to take risk with their capital?"

"Thank you for having me on today, Paula. I always say to women everywhere. Money is power. If you have no money, you have no chance in today's world."

"That's not true. Artists have a place in shaping society," I talk back to the screen.

"Tell yourself that if that makes you feel better. How will your novel change anything if it doesn't sell?" George chimes in.

"I can write something that sells. You watch," I say.

Shifting my position, I stretch out my arms and look around the room. There's a desk near the bar area. Feeling the urge to write, I walk over to the desk with my drink in hand. A quill and thick rough paper adorn the glossy finish. It all feels so antique. I put the quill against the parchment and write two words.

Road Trip.

That feels hokey, but that's what my novel represents. I want the title to convey the importance of the story and grab the readers' interests. The Road to Vegas? That sounds better. I don't think it's perfect, but it sounds good enough in my head. There. I have begun. After all this time, I finally have a title.

Chapter One...NYC

***

"Did you make any progress on your novel?" He pops out of nowhere as if he possesses powers of mist or fog.

I flinch. *I only have the title.* Blocking my mind are thoughts of spending sprees and shopping extravaganzas. The mere possibility I'm rich chokes the creative juice inside me.

"How could I? After all that's happened in the last day."

"To be honest, this is just the beginning." He stares into my eyes.

I shrug. It's hard to disagree with that. It's as if I'm trapped in a movie with no control.

He places another drink next to me and takes a position near the door. The channel switches on its own to a sports channel. It's a rebroadcast of an old baseball game, Game 6 of the World Series between the Boston Red Sox and the New York Mets.

"Why is this on?" I turn my head toward him.

"It's always on." Neither his voice nor expression changes.

"You're joking."

"You'll have to ask Ray."

The volume seems to go up, too. *"The Red Sox leads two to zero after the second inning and leads the series three to two in this best of seven..."*

"Fine," I sigh. This man has no answers. Rising from the desk, I take my drink and plop down on the sofa to watch.

George appears at my side with the remote.

I continue. "Um...do me a favor. Tell me what I need to know. Without giving away any details or facts you're not permitted to..."

He cuts me off. "Bottom line?"

"Yes." I'm pretty sure my eyes are twinkling with anticipation.

"Show me and the people watching you can handle it. Being rich."

"Well?" I ask. "Tell me what it means to be rich."

Taking his gaze off the TV screen, he retraces his steps to the bar. He pours a half glass of the same whiskey I'm drinking and downs it straight away.

He sighs. "It *means* doing anything necessary to increase your fortune. You won't be given the money unless you can make it grow. How can we

29

trust you when you haven't even shown the ability to *make* it, let alone keep it or increase it?"

That was not what I expected. These greedy bastards want assurances I'll become one of them. It seems he doesn't have the guts to tell me to quit writing. Perhaps he thinks that isn't necessary. The money will do that without any help from him. I can feel the influence on me already.

"I told you. I can write a book that *will* sell."

"Prove it to me and you can have the money," he snorts. Draining a second glass, he exits the room.

Running to catch up to him, I turn the TV off and follow him up the stairs to my private apartment. When I get to the dressing room, I sit on the safe and open Ray's letter. I read and re-read it for some time. I want the words to burn into my brain.

The promise I made to you on the day your father died...

A steady beeping sound from the surveillance monitor interrupts my train of thoughts. It's the same man from last night—the FBI agent. This guy just won't go away. What does he want? If George knows him, he can't be here for me. It must have something to do with Ray. He approaches the camera, looks directly into the lens, and waves. His mouths a word. He's saying my name.

He knows I'm here!

My heart sinks. I'm no safer in this mansion than on the road. Shaking, I grab a pen and start scribbling.

Mr. George,

I'll continue my journey to the west in search of gold to show you I am worthy. My novel can entertain enough to increase the fortune. I hope to retain the message and change the lives of women everywhere, for the proper measure of wealth resides within our souls, not in our bank accounts.

Also, I've decided to write a new story instead of the one of my childhood. Those days are an important part of my life, but some parts are best left in quiet graves. That baseball game reminded me of my father, and that put me in a foul mood. Survival means forgetting. Why can't I stop thinking about him and move on?

Who knows what I'll encounter on my journey? The uncertainty appeals to me. Will I make it to Vegas? Will I ever see Ray again?

We shall see, Mr. George.

Ella

NYC

Snow coats the hood of my car even as the engine runs, and the waves of cold seep through the windows. The urge to spend the day in a hotel watching movies passes without a fight. I exit the car with my backpack on my shoulder and swipe my card to feed the meter. With no specific plan or destination in mind, I allow myself to blend in with the pedestrian traffic on the sidewalk. The snowflakes land on my face as the storm slows to a mild yawn from the heavens.

My legs are tight and ache from the drive. Struggling to find traction on the slick cement, I slip a few times. Nobody seems to notice or look my way. I pull the flaps of my parka tighter around my face and check out the shops nearby. The sudden need for a cup of coffee swarms my senses. I spy a Dunkin Donuts at the end of the next block, which gives me the necessary jolt to move again.

After purchasing a coffee, I take a seat and lean my head over the cup so the steam can warm my face. Rubbing my hands together, I open the *Village Voice*, which I grabbed on my way in, to the calendar section. There must be something to do or see on this cold but pretty mid-January day. An elderly man in a filthy, tattered winter coat eyes me with hostility. Does he want me to buy him a cup of coffee or give him money for alcohol?

"What the hell are you staring at, tramp?" he growls, spit flying from his mouth.

Turning away in horror, I bury my head in the magazine. The words become a blur as the anger rushes into my cheeks. *Welcome to New York.* After a sip of coffee, I manage to calm down enough to spot the ad of a poetry reading. It isn't an open mic night, which is good since I'm in mortal terror of being forced to read. In many of my nightmares, I'm naked on stage with him, and he shakes his head in disappointment as I fail to utter a single, intelligible sentence—much less a poem.

I plug the address into my phone's map application and I realize it's a mere block or two from here. The problem is the time, which is hours away, and I need to find a diversion. Avoiding the man's glare, I stand and leave my table. Once outside, I can't help but smile. The snow has finally stopped, and the temperature climbed up a few degrees. Strange how such a little thing can change one's mood...

Using the subway application on my smartphone, I search for the quickest path to Washington Square Park, one of the attractions on my checklist. Slipping on the stairs, I stumble across the row of automated Metro Card dispensers. I load enough money into my card to avoid standing in lines all day. Rushing through the turnstile, I hurry toward the sound of the train.

A handsome, young NYPD officer tips his cap at me. I smile at him and board the train. When I'm safely in, I pull out my phone. Busy reading the description of the park, I fail to notice a man near me. Well, that is until he squeezes in beside me on the plastic bench. He appears to be a homeless man. I'm confused because there are many empty seats around us, and he's chosen to invade my space. It's quite unpleasant and unnecessary.

I smell a mix of dried sweat and alcohol. I try to lean as far away as I can, but I'm pinned against the exit pole and have no way to escape.

"Excuse me, sir, but can you please slide down a seat? You're crushing me against the pole," I plead in my sweetest, most innocent voice. *If he keeps touching me, I'll cut his fucking throat.*

I don't know what this man is capable of. He stares at me with his dark eyes. His brown hair, matted with grime and dirt, sticks out into every direction. To me, this is the look of pure insanity.

"I like the way you smell," he grunts, leaning closer.

In a panic, I turn my head and look around me. There are several passengers on all sides, but no one pays any attention to me or this man. His voice was so loud that it's impossible for anyone to have missed it.

"Sir, please!" I say. My voice is firm and loud. I hope and pray he'll leave me alone. In my mind, I form the prayer.

I can't stab him on this train. I can't stab him on this train. I can't...

Nope. He doesn't hear my prayers and pushes his face close to mine. I feel wetness on my skin. My stomach flips and turns as I realize he's licking my neck. A scream parts my lips, and my eyes snap open to see the man slinking away down the aisle.

Thankfully, a bell rings, and a voice announces my stop. Waiting for the doors to open, I fight the urge to cry and storm out of the train. After the short walk to the park, the incident seems to fade into nothingness. Oh, NYC.

The park teems with life: groups of students in circles tapping away at electronic devices, homeless people sleeping on benches, and couples walking hand in hand. These couples kiss and stare into the city. I locate an open bench and sit before anyone snags it, taking the center to discourage anyone from joining me. Pulling out my tablet, I open the word processor. While I wait for inspiration to strike, I follow the path of a young couple, a rather tall, older black man with a young, handsome blond man, obviously many years his junior.

"What are you writing?" I hear a man's voice coming from close to me.

I didn't see him approach and it startles me. I wonder if he read my words on the screen and snap the magnetic case over the tablet. This man looks about my age and is sporting a black leather jacket that is quite expensive. He smiles at me and sits next to me on the bench, forcing me to move to the side.

"Words," I reply with a smile but don't want to engage him in a conversation. Why is it that every time I begin writing, men pick that moment to hit on me? *Men. I swear they vex me on purpose.*

"You have a pretty smile," he says, giving no indication he saw my writing.

"Well, I thank you, sir. You are too kind."

When he leans closer, heat rises in my face. *Doesn't anybody in this damn city respect personal space?*

"Are you a writer?" he asks in a low voice.

"What makes you think that?"

"For one, you were writing just now. Second, you didn't notice me and were staring off into space watching the couple over there. It seemed to me like you were sketching them, so to speak."

I scan the park to see if anyone notices us, but it seems the world couldn't care less. I can't suppress a smile when I face him, and he grins back with his head tilted to the side. He's a looker. I wonder if he's going to ask me for coffee or something.

As if on cue, he leans in and whispers again. "Do you smoke?"

Not what I expected him to say. "I have my own cigarettes, but thank you."

He chuckles and wags a finger. His wide smile reveals his perfect, white teeth. "I did not mean cigarettes, pretty lady."

"Not to be rude, but even if I did smoke, I wouldn't rush off to do it with a stranger in NYC," I say, trying to end the conversation.

"Why not? You're a writer, correct? You came to the city for adventure. Don't chicken out now. Do it. Let's go smoke."

"I need more convincing than that. Tell me something about yourself." He reaches for my hand, but I pull away and wait for him to answer me.

"I'm in finance. Stocks."

"You don't say." Just the type of man George wants me to spend time with. And indeed, why not? I like his high cheekbones and kind eyes. He's quite right, I am looking for adventure to write about in my journal. "Fine, let's smoke. Do you have a place, or will we have to do it in my car?"

"We can do it in your car if that's what you want." He winks.

"Don't be a potty mouth, sir." I put my tablet into my backpack and stand. "Do you have a place or not?"

He puts his hand into mine, which shocks me, and begins walking south through the park. "I happen to have an apartment a few blocks away."

"Do you happen to have hot chocolate?" I try to ignore the tingling sensation rising in my belly as he wraps his arm around mine and squeezes my fingers.

With a nod, he leads me out of the park to the snow covered boulevard.

***

This city, which is said to be the very heartbeat of our country, confounds me. I'm led by a nameless man through the maze of buildings of untold wealth. We approach his apartment tenement that rises like an eyesore of poverty yet is surrounded alternately by beauty and squalor. How can such opulence lead to abject neglect?

I follow him up the stairs in near darkness, securing my foot on each creaking step before lifting myself higher. His abode turns out to be a third floor loft in a brick tenement building. At turns, it goes from drafty to sauna hot. One can find each condition by moving a mere span of feet from the kitchen to the living room. And there's no definitive line drawn to see where one begins or the other ends.

The place contains almost nothing in the way of furniture or decoration like paintings, posters, or other adornments on the bare concrete walls. Taking off my knit hat, I plop down on the tattered brown faux leather couch. I sift through old magazines on a glass coffee table as he busies himself in the kitchen. The scent of the hot chocolate fills the room.

"I'm Robert, by the way." He hands me a steaming cup of real hot chocolate instead of prepackaged ones.

Sipping it, I watch him. He takes a seat quite closely and presses his leg against my own.

"And yes, I prefer Robert. Not Robby, Bob, Rob, or whatnot. Robert is a poet's name."

"And are you a poet, Robert, not Rob?" The warmth from his leg travels to mine.

He chuckles and coaxes wild stands of hair over my ear with a finger. I wait nervously for what he might do or say next. Though it feels as if I'm about to shrink into the couch under him, I manage to lean back only an inch or two into the cushion.

"No," he says before jumping from the couch and striding into the bedroom. He returns quickly with a glass pipe and passes it to me.

Seeing that it's packed, I spark the lighter and feel a warm, mellow glow flow through my body. Placing my head against the couch, I close my eyes. A lone trumpet sounds from a nearby speaker. Silently, we listen as the slow jazz ballad plays, each taking time with the bowl without speaking or engaging the other.

"What's your name?"

The machine changes the music selection.

Without opening my eyes or reacting to his hand on my leg, I tell him, "Ella."

"Pretty name. Tell me something, beautiful young thing with the lovely name. What are you doing in the city by yourself?" His words are slow but playful.

"I didn't know I needed a chaperone."

Moving his hand higher on my leg, he inches toward me slowly but steadily, making more contact with my body. "It is a dangerous place. A lot can happen to a pretty girl like you." He slides a hand under my sweater and teases my stomach with his fingers.

I giggle. "Dangerous, you say? Like what you're about to do my body?"

Pulling my head onto his lap, he lets out a slow, quiet laugh, "Not exactly."

"I don't think so," I say as he tries to force my hands into his pants.

"Do it for the story." He laughs again.

I pull away from him, lean against the other arm of the couch, and place my legs on him. "I'm sorry, sir. I don't do that. Not even in a story. But you can rub my feet if you wish."

"What kind of adventure will that be?" Though he protests, he pulls my socks off and begins to trace his fingers along the arch of my foot.

"It will be a story women will want to read. A gorgeous stranger treated me well without taking advantage. Perhaps, the gentleman took said girl to a nice restaurant in Times Square."

Still laughing, he touches me with soft, slow strokes that makes me close my eyes once more. "We might be able to negotiate such an *adventure*."

Taking the bowl from the table, I spark a deep hit and stretch, enjoying the feel of the music along with his touch and the warmth against my skin. When he begins to climb on top of me again, I do not protest or open my eyes, not wanting to fight his lips from tasting mine.

"You are beautiful," he breathes into my mouth.

I don't respond. I just let my mind drift into story, seeing the words print on the paper of my mind.

He undresses her with care, kissing every inch of skin he exposes. Light, tender kisses make her arch against his touch. Time drips as he runs fingers over her body, bringing a pleasurable chill down her spine. She puts her arms around his neck as he lowers himself onto her, pressing lips against his neck and whispering into his ear, "Be gentle, good sir, for I have not known a man in this way for a year. And that didn't end well at all."

***

The boy, or Robert the wannabe poet, didn't take me to dinner after all. I shouldn't find that to be a surprise, seeing as I gave him what he wanted ahead of time. So, I stand in Times Square as darkness descends. As the snow falls on the tourists and the screeching of tires and horns crash into my ears, I'm not sure what I should be feeling at this moment. I can't help being underwhelmed, or at least not left feeling awed at being on this spot where so many millions have walked before me.

The pushy masses don't allow proper time to take it all in. Everyone seems in a rush to take their guided tour. Debating between taking pictures that I won't look at or trying to secure a place to stay for the night, I can't shake the thoughts of what happened this afternoon. To be honest, the events fill me with emotion. Robert is only the second man

I've had sex with in my adult life. I won't put an asterisk on the number like that baseball move about Roger Maris I found so appealing because I don't feel like discussing my father right now. I will, I promise, in due time.

In both cases, the event only happened a single time (and seeing as I'm leaving the city quite soon, I can't see how that won't be the case in this instance as well). Saying that I have only had sex two times since turning 18 is a little embarrassing. It makes me feel like a child instead of an adult. Indeed, I told him I don't do *that*, and in truth, I never have done it. I don't even know how. I feel even more embarrassed that I just lay there and let him do as he pleased. It was like when I was young and scared, waiting for it to be over. When will I learn to enjoy sex?

This city is beautiful; there can be no debate. As I look to the heavens and watch the snow fall in a rainbow of colors against the skyline, I feel the presence of words forming. The constant, comfortable companion in my brain does the writing, converting the collected images into sentences. How many have stood here looking up at that giant Coca Cola sign and wondered how on earth did they get it up there? I'm aware of cranes and other things, but it's so high that I'd like to believe that Superman himself placed it atop that building.

Pedestrians keep pushing me, making it difficult for me to maintain a spot long enough to take in an adequate view. Why are people always in such a rush? Do they always have a plan and destination? A few readers have commented on my blog saying there isn't much of a plot to my story. To be honest,

41

I want it that way. I want to experience this country, not just plow my way across or hit a set series of dots to say that I've done it. I want it to happen naturally, for lack of a better way of expressing my intentions.

A voice catches my attention. I spin in the direction of the sound and find a policeman with his hands on his hips. From the way he's watching me, I think he might believe I'm either lost or a runaway.

"Can I help you? Are you lost or in need of assistance?" *Why, just because I'm a girl alone in the big city? Fucking men.*

"No, Officer. I'm just enjoying the view. So pretty, isn't it?"

He doesn't even pretend to look around, his eyes remaining glued to mine. "This city is a shithole," he grunts.

With that, he melts back into the crowd. What made him so bitter that he can't enjoy this perfect winter evening? To me, with the snow falling and a small breeze carrying the scent of a local Italian restaurant across the plaza, the night is truly divine. I want to hug it against my chest and bottle it...if only that were possible. I feel a slight chill coming over me even though I'm wearing a knit cap and an adequate winter jacket. Where will I go tonight?

Taking my phone out, I hit a button to access a stored number before I can change my mind. The line buzzes several times on the other end before I hear an answer.

"What can I do for you, Ella?" George asks.

"I'm in Times Square and I want to do something."

George recites an address, which is close to my current location. "Give your name to the man at will call, and everything will be taken care of, I assure you."

"What show?" I begin to ask, but the line goes dead.

With a shrug, I put my phone in my pocket and begin walking the short journey to the theatre. Snow floats in the air and time seems to slow. Bits of conversation and the squeal of brakes mix together to form a mad score.

Arriving at the address, I look up and see the marquee. *Cinderella.* I bet George is winking at me from Connecticut. I wait in line, pulling my jacket more tightly around my shoulders. When it's my turn, I give my name to the old woman behind the thick glass. She smiles and motions for me to follow an elderly gentleman in a tuxedo.

Without a word, the man leads me through the theatre. There are tourists taking pictures of the stage and gazing at it all in wonder. The man takes a small staircase, which ends with a door. Opening it, he ushers me inside a private box seat, the farthest from the stage and the one with the best view of all the box seats.

"Can I get a drink?" I ask.

"You shall be served without delay," he says before exiting, leaving me alone in the box.

Taking a seat in one of the four chairs facing the stage, I watch the action below with interest. People push and jostle for seats while holding drinks and other refreshments bought at the concession stand.

Within a few minutes I hear a tap at the door and a man enters with a tray. He places a glass on a table near my chair and fills it with a shaken martini. With a small smile, he exits without a word. The lights dim three times, and I feel a rush of excitement come over me. The show will begin soon.

CINDERELLA

The lights flash, the music begins, and the curtain rises to signal the start of the show. As I get ready to watch, the door opens, and the Hispanic man who's been following me enters. Without a word he nods and takes the seat next to me. The waiter brings another martini and exits, leaving me and the FBI agent alone.

"No lack of irony here," he whispers, smiling but with eyes on the stage.

I assume he means this play, but I don't respond.

"Why are you in a box? The view leaves a lot to be desired."

I take a mouthful of martini and swallow, closing my eyes as the alcohol numbs my mouth and relaxes my nerves.

"A rich older man leaves a castle to a pretty young girl. There is something of a fairytale in your story."

It's obvious that he's fishing for information but isn't asking the right questions. And I'm not going to help him. So, he left me a castle. Big deal. Sipping my drink, I watch a girl wearing a ball gown sing about her woe-begotten life.

"Why did he leave Holden Farms to you?" he asks again.

And again, I ignore him. My gaze is fixed on the spectacle on the stage, which teems with women in many colors of dresses and men in dazzling white tuxedos. It feels like a formal ball to me, not that I've ever been to one or have a clue. After the scene, the curtain drops, and I rise from my seat.

"The ladies' room," I say to him, hoping he won't follow.

"Wait, I have something for you." He pulls a thick envelope from his leather jacket and extends it my way. I see the remnants of my early writing that was taken by the authorities when my father died. "How did you get this?"

"Stay. I might tell you."

No, I'm not sticking around for him to finish. I push my way into the hallway. To my happiness, he stays in the box. I run as fast as my heels allow toward the front entrance. Signaling the man that helped me find my seats, I pant.

"What's the fastest way to the subway?"

"Are you not staying for the second half of the show?"

I wave a hand at him in impatience and push my way outside, retracing my steps north. A wave of fear passes over me when I realize that I might be late for the poetry reading. Following the directions on my phone to the subway, I push my way into a tide of traffic.

Walk seven minutes along 7th Avenue to reach E Subway train local service.
92nd Street Y

At the entrance of the lobby, an older man wearing a grey sweater, glasses, and holding a clipboard approaches me. His palms gesture me to stop. Pausing near a row of pictures documenting the writers who performed through the years, I wait for him to reach me. He stops close enough for me to smell his Old Spice aftershave.

"You can't be here. The reading already started," he whispers, hand gripping my upper arm.

My eyes find his fingers, and I roll my eyes. "I saw an ad. It's an open reading. I want to read."

"Listen. It's an open reading in spirit with preference given to those that donate to the center."

Of course, he wants money. It's NYC. I should've known. "How much?"

"Donations start at one hundred dollars, but like I've said, the line-up is set..."

"I will offer ten thousand dollars," I say, not letting him finish.

Brown eyes framed by thick reading glasses scan me. Taking a pen from his pocket, he makes a scratch on the sheet. "Make a check..."

"I'm bringing cash. Take it or leave it." Before he can answer, I open my backpack. Grapping a few wrapped bundles of hundred dollar bills, I stack the money on his clipboard and smile. "Now, tell me where to read."

With newfound confidence, I follow him into the hall. Down a steep ramp toward the stage, some fifty people fill the first few rows, watching a woman read poetry. Eyes follow us, forcing the woman to stop performing. All ears listen to the sweater cop speak to an important looking woman near the stage.

"We've been through this before, Claire. Big donors get to read even at a late hour or at the cost of a student-reader."

Student-reader? Does that mean someone who hasn't made a donation? No matter. The woman yields, and ushers the redhead off the stage. I wait for her to move beyond my position before I put my heel on the stage steps. Hoping not to trip, I make a slow path toward the podium, stepping over wires taped to the stage.

A hush falls over the room and I'm ready to freak out. I don't even know what I'll read. Tapping the microphone in a sham of checking if it's on, I'm sad to find out it works. Eyes stare, and moments expire, but I am no closer to speaking. Placing the backpack on the floor, I remove my journal and leave it on the podium. I open the pack of papers given to me the FBI agent, and my eyes find a title.

ROUTINE

Late night is my favorite time of day. When he is sleeping and the TV is off, I can breathe. All is silent. I am left to myself. Not even he can bother me. He fell asleep on the couch hours ago, giving me time. There are those moments before he passes out in front of the tube. I wonder if I'll go insane. I can't even watch television without a hassle. I wish he'd leave me alone.

What I wouldn't give for a good book right now. I wish I had a book to read, so I wouldn't have to think so much. Some days, all I do is think of all that is happening and wonder. I wonder why my life is like this and why Mother went away. I wish my favorite writers would write faster. I read all they write and read them again and again, but my eyes get tired. And I end up sitting and thinking, thinking and sitting, and waiting, waiting, waiting for sleep.

Every night, I go through the same routine with few exceptions. After dinner, I do my homework for two hours. My father has this idea that I should study for two hours. I don't know where he got the idea that 7th graders were supposed to study for two hours, probably from some paper sent home from the school, but he thinks it is an unwritten law. He makes me sit at my desk for two hours even if I finish early.

"Read something," he'll yell up the stairs if I ask if I can watch television. "At least, use all that damned

shit I bought you. That computer wasn't fucking cheap you little, ungrateful witch."

It usually goes something like that for two hours. It is the same every night, except Friday and Saturday nights. I get to do the weekend homework on Sundays. And yes, he was nice enough to buy me a computer to do my writing. He says it cost him fifteen hundred dollars, but I know he stole the damn thing. On the nights I finish my homework early, I type in my computer journal like tonight. I like to rant and rave about school, but usually, I bitch about my dad. I never run out of things to say about him.

Well, back to the routine. I told you about the homework part. After I finish my homework, which he of course checks, I am allowed to watch exactly one hour of television. When he is in a good mood, I'm allowed to choose the shows. Those nights are rare, but when they occur, I take advantage. I turn it to MTV. He hates this channel. He sits next to me on the couch and grunts his disapproval.

He will even goes so far as to bash a song or two, but when he lets me control the set, he doesn't change the channel. He just sits there and watches right beside me. Sometimes, to show my gratitude, I'll lean my head on his shoulders. And on nights that he is really pleasant, I'll let him hold my hand. I may not get along with him, but since my mother died two years ago, he is all I have.

After I watch my hour of television, he tells me it's time to get ready for bed. Bedtime around this house for me is nine o'clock. I can't tell you how many hours I have spent arguing and pleading with him for a later bedtime, but he is stuck on his routines. Bedtime is nine o'clock. Sharp.

So, up the stairs to get ready for bed, which isn't a simple thing for me. I have to look my best. Imagine going to bed for the night with snarled hair! I won't have it. No. Not at all. I must groom with care. The routine will probably bore you, but here it is anyway.

First, I put on my pajamas. There is no sense in brushing your hair when you have to pull a shirt over your head! I brush my hair for ten minutes. I love the way the brush feels in my hair. I run the brush through from front to back again and again. One hundred times. After I brush my hair, I tend to my nails. I clip them, file them, and wonder how they would look with those fancy nail polishes I see advertised on television. My dad won't let me wear nail polish, or makeup for that matter. He says it would make me look like a tramp. I don't want to look like a tramp like that girl Jessie at school, but I do want to paint my nails. It might make me feel more grown-up.

After I do my nails, I go to the bathroom. I brush my teeth. I can hear him now saying five minutes, floss, and use the mouthwash. He likes me to use spearmint kind. He is very particular about my breath. Then I wash my face. I go back to my room, check myself in the mirror, and hop into bed with the light on. Dad always shuts it off for me. I count the minutes until he raps on the door.

One, two, three quick, light knocks.

"Are you sleeping?" he asks every night.

"No, Daddy."

He opens the door, shuts off the light, and gets into bed with me.

I walk from the stage, ignoring the silence, the absence of applause, and the glare of the man in the gray sweater. I rush out of there without a second thought. Walking north after leaving the theater, I pass the hotel. I'm making a straight line for my car and leaving this city as soon as possible. I don't know why I read that piece, but I need forget it before the dreams start again.

HELLO, STRANGER

The traffic remains sparse on I-80, which I plan on taking all the way to Cleveland. The constant litany of thoughts about the last few days of volcanic change in my life clutters my mind. I tap my fingers on the steering wheel to distract myself. A blast of frigid air snaps me to reality when I roll down my window at a toll booth. I turn up the volume of the music, "… And Justice for All" by Metallica, as I rejoin traffic.

I dread stopping at highway rest stops for fast food, but it's an unavoidable travesty of a road trip. Being forced to eat at the Golden Arches from time to time seems inevitable. As I look in the rearview mirror to negotiate a lane change, I spot a billboard sign of that bastion of American cuisine. I also notice a gray BMW that looks familiar. *Did I see that car in NYC?* Signaling, I change lanes and feel a tightness in my stomach. The BMW does the same.

It does appear that the car is following me, and a small measure of panic rises in my veins. The turn for the rest stop approaches, and I veer into the lane at the last possible moment. No luck. My shadow follows without a hitch. The car parks very near to mine, but nobody exits the car while I make my way inside the group of buildings. I take quite a long time tending to business. Before getting in line for a hamburger and shake, I spend extra time in the bathroom, fixing my hair and grabbing more energy drinks and snacks from the store.

Under normal circumstances, I'd take my meal to-go, but I want ample time to remove all doubt. If the car is still there when I go back outside, I'm definitely being followed. Throwing the remnants in the trash, I wrap a pink scarf around my neck and push my way outside. My feet move briskly toward my car.

As I suspected, the BMW sits in the same spot. The driver's side door opens, and a giant man with wild brown hair and thick beard looks up at me. As his dark eyes lock with mine, I can't help thinking I've seen him somewhere, which is odd because I couldn't forget a man of his size. How tall is he, six and a half feet? He takes a large bite of a chocolate bar while his eyes study me. I stare at him before getting into my car, having no reason to hurry.

"Hi." I wave at him as I stand there shivering.

Ignoring me, he finishes the candy and drops the wrapper on the ground. Narrowing my eyes at him, I march over to pick up the trash and place it in the barrel near his car. We stare at each other. *I know your face.* I can't remember his name, but somehow he must be associated with Ray. There can be no other explanation.

A cold wind forces me to end the staring contest and get inside my car. I waste no time getting back on the interstate. No point in looking back since I know he'll be right behind me. The thought repeats in my mind while the radio begins to phase out between stations. What's your name? Shaking my head, I turn the knobs, looking for a new radio station and stop when I hear an urgent female voice reading the news.

"We begin with tragic news out of NYC where famed futures trader Robert Mustov was found murdered in his Manhattan apartment late Friday night. A victim of apparent domestic violence, police reports. An ex-girlfriend is in custody at this hour."

What the hell? Is it possible that he's the same Robert I met this afternoon? I dictate a voice text to George, asking for more information. The miles melt ahead as I check the phone every few minutes and close the distance to Cleveland. There's no response, and I discover that the car needs fuel. Slamming the wheel as I take the first exit I see, I pull into a gas station with a convenience store.

A small smile forces itself on my face as I see the BMW stop on the other side of the parking lot. After refueling, I go inside to purchase cigarettes and a bottle of wine.

The old man behind the counter will probably card me. It appears wine won't be on the menu tonight. With a sigh, I pay for my cigarettes and return to my car to see a sheet of paper under the wiper. The man leans against his car with arms crossed on his chest. Assuming he put it there for me to read it, I lift it up toward the street light to get a better view.

I will not hurt you, girl.
Mr. Brown

An image of him from my childhood flashes across my mind, but the memory disappears before I can pinpoint the exact day. I do remember you, sir. I enter the car and see something on the passenger's seat. It's a small black box containing a cell phone, a letter, and a few stacks of one hundred dollar bills.

Ella,
You must be more careful on your journey as this country is rife with danger. Mr. Brown will follow, at a discreet distance, to keep you out of too much trouble. There is a phone in case you need to get in touch with him, and the number programmed in for you. I took the liberty of giving you a spot of spending money. I hope you will not object. I do hope you are enjoying your trip.
Yours always,
Ray

When I press the letter against my face, I can almost smell his cologne. I hug it against my chest before an idea lights a lamp inside my mind. Peeling a bill from the stack, I jump from the car and walk towards Mr. Brown. I extend my arm and hold out the money.

"Go get me a bottle of wine," I say with a coy smile.

"I don't—"

I cut him off. "Don't make me beg, Mr. Brown."

He pauses and tilts his head. "Do you remember?"

No. I can't remember. His face seems familiar, but I can't pull the memory from my mind. He walks into the store and soon returns with a bottle. I can't hide the corner of my lips going upward as I see that it's a bottle of soda. Not knowing what else to do, I take it and get back to my car. Before I shut the door, I face him once more. "See you in Cleveland, sir."

The years in the nut house burned the habit onto my brain. Saying sir to every man comes automatically. How long before I can break that habit? Or can I use it to my advantage? Thoughts and more thoughts.

***

The clock reads 7:25 as I enter the city limits, and I wonder about the location of Mr. Brown. Traffic thickens in the main boulevard toward downtown. I turn onto W322 and begin to look around for hotels. Parking in an open spot, I wait for my phone to load a list of places with available rooms and take the opportunity to look at the skyline, which seems small compared to NYC. Before the page can finish, I find a text message from Mr. Brown and can't help smiling.

I secured you a room at the Ritz-Carlton. You are welcome.
Mr. Brown

Showoff. Not that I don't appreciate the gesture. When I type the name into the map application and wait for directions, the voice feature begins to dictate to me. I arrive in mere minutes as the hotel stands quite close to W322. The hotel overlooks the Cuyahoga River that seems to shine tonight. I follow the sight as long as possible before entering, letting a valet take my car and a bellhop carry my bags.

The lobby sings with wood accents and hushed tones of tan and gold. I feel happy but also really hungry. When and where will I be able to get dinner? The bellboy opens the door and leads me into the room. My eyes widen at the spacious affair that contains three rooms with large windows looking out onto the city. Putting a hundred dollar bill in the boy's hand, I'm left to myself again. I notice a rectangular box on the bed and skip over to it in spite of the exhaustion and cramping in my legs from the drive.

Lifting the cover reveals a flowing silk dinner dress that makes me gasp. The green dress is sleeveless with a low-cut back, and the front is covered with emerald-colored stones and silver lining. A note falls from the box as I lift the dress. Wow, that's a sexy dress. I think for a moment that Mr. Brown will see me in it...but push it from mind and read the note.

You still have time for dinner if you hurry. They are expecting you.

Yours,
Ray

Squealing with delight, I run for the bathroom and jump into the shower. Am I to dine alone, or will the mysterious Mr. Brown be my chaperone for the evening? I feel anticipation pulsing in my veins, but take time to shave without cutting my legs. Putting on the dress, I love the way the silk kisses my skin. I slide my feet into the black pumps next to the bed and grab the matching purse before leaving the room.

As I pull open the door, I slam into Mr. Brown, who's standing there in a black suit with a smirk. It looks funny with his thick beard hanging over the tie, but I think the jacket fits him well at least. We both take a moment to look over the other. He extends his arm to me and escorts me to dinner. The Captain seems to be expecting our arrival and leads us to a table in silence, so I check out the room.

A chandelier hangs over the grand piano in a corner. Right away, we are led to a table with blue-backed chairs and a vase of roses as a centerpiece. A waiter approaches with a bottle of wine, which I guess Mr. Brown ordered in advance. Pouring a glass for both of us, he makes a small bow before leaving us alone.

"Quite an unexpected surprise," I say, smiling and sipping the wine.

"Aren't surprises always unexpected?" he answers.

Ooh, aren't we grumpy pants.

"Can you at least fake pleasantries, sir?"

"I am not paid to fake it with you," he growls.

"What exactly are you paid to do?" I sip more wine and study him while a hint of anger build up in my cheeks.

"None of your business."

The waiter approaches the table to tell us the specials. I don't hear a thing and stare at Mr. Brown, trying to get him to look at me. Feeling the waiter pause, I turn to him and notice a rather plain looking middle-aged man with silver hair looking back at me.

"I'll take whatever he's having, please."

Mr. Brown grunts and orders Pan Roasted Salmon for both of us.

I pause to let the waiter leave before I speak. "I will talk with Ray about this. Somehow, I'd bet he wants you to be nicer to me."

I hear his teeth grinding together and smile. He finishes the wine in an angry gulp and slams the glass on the table. The waiter scurries over to pour while Mr. Brown glares at me with his jaw clenched and little spots on his forehead bunched with effort.

"There won't be a need to call Ray. As it stands, I don't work for him anymore."

Oh, wait a minute.

Putting down my glass, I assume he will add to that statement and wait for him to continue. Instead, he glares, offering no further explanation.

"Okay, fine. I'll ask. Tell me who you work for."

"You, Ella."

What? Did I hear him say that? "Care to explain that?"

He turns away and stare at the floor. I can almost hear the gears turning inside his mind.

"Ray gave me to you."

"I don't understand. Like a possession?"

Lifting his eyes to meet mine, he stares for a while. From the corner, a man begins to play soft jazz on the piano. We're still silent as the waiter arrives with dinner, and Mr. Brown polishes off another glass in a gulp.

"Slow down, sir."

The man seems to swill alcohol like it's water. Ignoring me, he devours his food and finishes the plate in mere minutes. While nibbling my food, I stare at him. Ordering another bottle of wine, he leans back in the chair.

"Don't ask me to repeat it. You're a writer. I'm sure you can figure it out for yourself."

Meanwhile, I follow a small scar that runs from the corner of his right eye down the side of his cheek before disappearing into his thick beard. I'm curious about how he got it and also what he looks like clean shaven. Despite his personality that needs a lot of work, I do find him handsome in a rough sort of way. *For a caveman.*

"You will stay in my room. I don't want to spend the night wondering where you're lurking."

"I will not," he says.

Slapping the table harder than I intended brings stares from a few nearby tables. I look away from him and tend to my dinner, not wanting to let him spoil it for me. The salmon pairs well with the white wine and calms me as I breathe in the scent of lemon and cinnamon. I smile at him and sip my wine.

"Yes, you will, sir."

Without answering me, he signals for the waiter. "I'll take scotch, something good. Two glasses."

That will do for an answer. My smile grows wider. It can't be this easy to subdue such a big, strong man. Can it? The scotch arrives, and he pushes a glass toward me. I've never tasted scotch. I can't help thinking it smells like vomit. People like this? I watch him take a mouthful and do the same. I spit some out as it burns like fire on my tongue. Some I do manage to swallow feels like hot spice going down my throat.

He chuckles and finishes his glass, slamming it on the table. "Do you like it?"

"It's not as bad as I thought," I say, coughing.

"Rare for a girl to like scotch."

I glare at him. I hate that crap. "Don't call me a girl."

Still chuckling, he signals for another drink. This man must be a total drunkard.

"You *are* a girl."

"Maybe to an old man like you." *He argues, but his eyes ravage me.*

"I'm only a year younger than Ray, Ella."

"What did you say?"

"Nothing." He slams the new drink down in one pass.

It's obvious that he's getting drunk. As his eyes are gaining a hint of red, he leans forward against the table. I wait for a response, but he signals for the check.

"Don't worry, I will leave you alone. I prefer a woman, not a girl."

"Hey, what about dessert?" I grumble.

After he throws down a handful of cash, we walk out of the restaurant. I hook an arm through his to keep him from stumbling rather than an attempt to flirt.

"Somehow, I bet you will change your mind, Mr. Brown. Men talk big until the lights go out."

"You're scrawny. Not much in the way of tits or ass. Blunt enough for you?"

What an asshole. I will make him regret those words. No matter what it takes, I shall have him.

As I open the door to my room, he staggers toward a couch and collapses on top of it. Within moments, his snoring begins. I shake my head. It certainly won't happen tonight. Goodnight, Mr. Brown.

ROCK AND ROLL

My head throbs when I open my eyes, and I find myself alone in the master bedroom of the suite. Rubbing at my temples, I swing my legs onto the floor and stagger into the bathroom. I let the water run and stick my head under the faucet to wet my lips. *I shouldn't have forced that scotch down.*

From my purse, I grab some aspirin from my travel medicine kit and chew slowly. The metallic bitterness overwhelms my taste buds. I don't remember changing into sweatpants, but it doesn't matter. At this point, I don't care that I look like a mess in only a tube top with no bra. Mr. Brown can deal with it. When I stumble into the living room, I see an empty couch. That's not a surprise, but he left a note on the table.

I'll be back.
Mr. Brown

Such eloquence. He must be a writer. That reminds me to make notes about last night. His words can't be lost. I sit at a desk against the wall and start writing in my notebook. Just then, the door opens behind me. Staying busy but aware of his presence, I continue to write everything I can remember of the dinner—especially the edgy conversation. A burst of pine scent fills my nose as he leans against me and tries to look at my writing. He places a cup of coffee on the desk next to me.

Aww, he did something sweet. Fighting the urge to look at him, I flip the cover and take a sip.

Immediately, I spit it out. "I hate sugar in my coffee."

"Do you think I give a shit?" He grimaces, pulling his face close enough for me to feel his body heat on my skin.

A shiver runs down my spine as I push the coffee away. "I don't care if you do or not. You will get me another one, *cream only.*"

Spinning the chair, he grips my shoulders, and mouths each word for emphasis. "I will not."

"You will."

His eyes bore into mine, and flashes of emotion pass over his pupils. Our stare grinds the air to a halt with the lone sound of the chair creaking when I try to move away from him.

"If you remembered me, you might not be so quick to give orders."

So, he is a killer type. What does that mean? "Fine, we can get coffee when we go out today."

Chuckling, he releases my shoulders and sits on a recliner a few feet away. He takes a pack of cigarettes from his pocket and lights one. "I'm not going anywhere today. I'll buy a bottle of whiskey and do my best to finish it. You're welcome to join me or not."

"You're taking me to the Rock and Roll Hall of Fame." I'm going to have to break him of fighting me on every little thing.

He coughs and slaps his knee in a laughing fit. After a while, he settles down enough to respond. "I am not a fucking tour guide."

Jumping from the chair, I stomp over to him and grab the cigarettes. I take a long, hard drag, glaring and seething. He continues to laugh, which only enrages me more with each second. Reaching into his pocket, he hands me an MP3 player.

"You'll find Zeppelin, The Beatles, The Stones, and others. Play some music, look at pictures online, and it'll be almost as good as being there."

"You're a real piece of work. I'm going to guess your Facebook status says single."

"Only losers use Facebook."

"Do me a favor. Keep your opinions to yourself, and go get that damned whiskey," I say, leaving the room with my feet slapping loudly on the hardwood of the kitchen area.

Sitting on a stool and swinging my foot in irritation, I smoke in silence. Thoughts race around my head. I see him putting on a leather jacket and heading out.

"Bring back another coffee, please, Mr. Brown." I put on a smile, which he catches a glimpse of before the door shuts.

Opening my notebook, I jot down a few sentences but can't continue. It occurs to me that I don't have time, so I leave the notebook open on the desk. A bath is needed to clear my head and take the sting out of this growing hangover. Grabbing a bottle of water from the fridge, I walk into the shower room, shedding my clothes. There's a part of me that wants him to see them and leave me alone for a while.

Running the water, I pour bath liquid. The scents of vanilla and brown sugar fills the room. I dip my toe and decrease the temperature. After testing one more time, I slide into the tub and lean my head against the pile of face towels along the railing. I can relax, hearing the pleasant sound of bubbles forming and popping as I stir the water.

I love baths. Maybe since my father forbade me because he said baths waste water. The man didn't like to spend money on anything besides alcohol. The feeling of the warm water is pleasant enough that memories of him can't ruin the moment.

The door slams, and I know he's back. The opening chords of "Whole Lotta Love" come from the living area moments before the door swings open. Mr. Brown enters, holding a few large bags from a local department store. He comes up to the edge of the tub and displays the items on the floor. I see a bag of coffee, a container of cream, and a coffeemaker. They seem quite expensive.

"Do you mind? I am trying to bathe."

"I don't mind at all." He smiles, looking at my feet that are sticking out of the water. Starting with his jacket, he starts to strip down to his boxers.

"What are you doing?"

"You left your notebook open. Seems you want a bit of attention." He laughs, pushing down his boxers to reveal his massive cock. It hangs low on his leg and swings as he puts a giant foot into the tub.

"Don't you dare," I yell, pushing at him, but he must three times my size. It's a useless affair, trying to keep him out.

He slides in next to me, lifts my body, and puts me on top of his. I kick and scream to escape, but it proves futile.

"Let me go, asshole!"

"I thought you wanted to *get me no matter what.* This is your chance."

"Don't quote my words if you don't understand what I'm writing."

"I understand quite well what you need," he whispers, rubbing my body against his thing, which grows thicker by the second.

"You don't understand anything. Now, let me go." When his hands release me, I spring from the tub, almost tripping on the packages on the floor while reaching for a towel. "After you're done we are going to see the museum."

I slam the door and storm into the bedroom to change. This will be a long day.

***

Mr. Brown's bath takes longer than mine did, and this allows me to have plenty of time to make notes on the next chapter. I wonder how my perception of the Rock and Roll Hall of Fame will match with reality when I see and hear it for myself. When I'm almost done with my work, he exits the bathroom with a hotel robe, not in any way looking ready to go out into the city. His robe opens while he hovers over me, trying to peek at the page. And he's naked. *Great, we will never leave at this rate.*

"Are you writing about me again or your father this time, perhaps?"

"Buzz off and go get ready, Mister."

"I have one question. Then we can go," he says.

Scanning his eyes, I search for any hint of sincerity. "Ask."

Sitting on a recliner close to the desk, he lights a cigarette and crosses his legs. "How much of your story is real?"

"Excuse me, but I won't answer that."

He takes a drag with a smug little grin pushing into his beard. I can hear lips smacking each time he puts the cigarette to his mouth, and it annoys me.

"Yes, you will."

After putting out the cigarette, he walks toward me. Leaning down, he pulls an object out of his pocket that I hear before I see. Metal slaps across my left wrist and before I can react, and he binds the other cuff to the chair. Laughing, he kisses me on top of the head like I'm a small child.

"You *will* unlock these handcuffs." I try to be stern, but the farce doesn't carry. My voice sounds hollow and thin.

"Answer my question. How much of the story is true, and how much are you embellishing?"

Doing my best to kill him dead with my eyes, I grip the chair and grit my teeth. I know he won't release me until I give him what he wants. Grunting, I lean back in the chair, crossing my legs at the ankles.

"I'm telling it as it happened. Detail for detail."

Letting out a whistle, he sits once again and lights another cigarette. This time, he adjusts his robe to cover himself. Opening the bottle of whiskey next to him, he pours a large tumbler full and sips at it as if he were waiting for me to continue.

"The way you describe the relations with your father makes me think it was voluntary at some point."

He might as well have slapped me. Tears fill my eyes. *You will regret saying that, Mr. Brown.* "I'm sorry my story doesn't fit the pre-conceived box you want it to fit into, but I can only tell it as it happened."

"Do you think your actions might have contributed to the abuse?"

"No, you didn't." I strain against the cuffs, trying to stand. I want to lift the chair, but it weighs too much. "Funny. I hear that same crap from every rapist. She dressed like a slut, or she was asking for it. There are a million variations of how to say you're a piece of shit."

Shrugging at my outburst, he sips the whiskey and holds out the glass to me. I nod and watch him pour a second glass and place it on the desk before resuming his position.

"I'm not trying to anger you. Only point out that you seemed to enjoy it."

"Oh, my...you must be a Republican. It can't be rape if the woman doesn't kick and scream. That's the basic message. Only *legitimate* rape counts, eh?"

"Relax. Don't get crazy on me. Take a drink and settle down, toots."

"What did you call me?" I scream before pounding the drink in one pass.

Laughing, he gets up and turns on the music, which turns out to be a jazz piece by John Coltrane, a live version of "Naima." "This man pioneered free jazz, one of the great musical movements of the last century."

Whiskey spreads warmth through me and down to my legs. *Why is he telling me this?* We sit in silence as the song plays. The song changes to Coltrane's hit song "My Favorite Things" as he sets his glass aside and approaches me again.

"I want to know if you enjoyed it."

Taking a deep breath, I try to gain control of my emotions. "Some of it. Life isn't black and white like you want it to be. There isn't a clear line between good and evil. If it were only that simple, we might be able to stomp out all the bad."

Grabbing my notebook, he opens it to a blank page and hands me the pen. "Write that. Put that in the story. You have to tell readers everything."

I put the pen to paper and write as he demands, hoping it'll get him to release me.

While I can't help looking back on the tragic events with regret and sadness, there were times with my father that I enjoyed, cherished even. He was all I had.

Turning the notebook to show him what I wrote, I wait to see if he will approve. He shrugs and returns to the chair, changing the music selection to a Rolling Stones song, "Sympathy for the Devil." "It's almost like being there."

"You complete *shit.*"

He bellows laugher and spits a generous amount of whiskey on the carpet. Still laughing as he pours more into his glass, his lip curls in an imitating smile. His foot taps along with the beat. Singing along, I can't help wondering what else he plans for me today.

THE SEDUCTION OF MR. BROWN

"This will not make for a good chapter, being chained to a desk," I say. *The wrong one of us is tied up, asshole.*

Instead of replying, he just sits and stares at me, sipping a glass of whiskey. His eyes scan my body. The intensity makes me feel naked. Rising, he approaches, fills my glass, and puts the bottle on the desk. Again, he stands so close I can feel his body heat.

"I know what type of story you wish to write." Pressing himself against me, he takes the pen and writes a few words in my notebook.

I will take you.

My mind swims to consider the implications. A shiver runs down my legs when his hand grazes my arm. I drink to settle my nerves and lift my eyes to meet his gaze.

"Do it," I blurt out. *I don't believe he will do it.*

Gripping my hair, he leans close to me and grins. "Be careful, girl."

I freeze, anticipating his next move. After a few seconds, he releases me and stands. I wink at him and take another sip of whiskey.

"Men are all talk."

"Is that a fact?"

Without waiting for my reply, he lifts the chair, carries it into the bedroom, and places it against the bed. Pulling me up, he lays me on the edge of the bed on my stomach, gently pressing my face into the mattress. I try to lift my arm, but the chair weighs too much. He pins my other arm under my body. With a large hand, he parts my legs and runs his fingers under my dress. I go limp and enjoy the feel of his rough skin gripping mine.

"What are you going to do with me, sir?"

"Be quiet, girl," he growls, bending down and kissing the inside of my thigh.

I shiver, expecting something rougher perhaps. "Make me, sir."

Lifting my legs, he yanks my dress off my body in one pull, leaving only a pair of silk panties as defense. His hands caress as thick lips make a journey along my ankles and calves. A blast of heat carrying his scent flows over me. I smile when he begins to massage my thighs and press his lips against my lower back.

"Oh, sir, you are right, I must be careful around you. You might pamper me to *death*," I moan, turning and winking at him. Still smiling, I push back against him. "Now, that's more like it."

Grunting, he pulls away and starts rubbing my feet. I sigh with disappointment and lift my waist, trying to lure him on again.

"You're a tease," he groans.

"I can assure you I'm not, but if you feel that way, why don't you spank me, sir?"

His hands pause, and I feel him watching me. Slowly, his palm runs over my leg, and with a quick motion, and he brings it down against my ass. "Do not push me."

"Or what, sir? I think me being restrained might be good for you, not the other way around."

Laughing, he returns to tracing my skin with his fingertips, starting on the soles of my feet and up the back of my leg. His thumb rubs a wet spot on my panties. Again, I push back, but his hand dances out of reach.

"And I'm the tease? Untie me. Don't be scared."

"Do you ever shut up?"

Helplessly, I giggle and shake my head vigorously in the negative. "Please unlock these cuffs. Are you man enough?"

"Perhaps I will. You think it's possible for me to be scared of you?"

Clearing my throat, I enunciate with care, "I am the most dangerous person in this room, sir."

Bursting into laugher, he looks away from me. "You don't even know what you are yet."

Letting his words ring in my mind for a few moments, I wonder what he really thinks of me. He does have a point. I don't know what I am. I have killed, but am I...no, I don't want to go there right now.

"Be that as it may, give me the key."

Shrugging, he reaches into his robe for the key and inserts it into the lock. As the handcuff falls away, I rub my wrist before flipping onto my back and sitting on the bed.

"Sit in the chair." I push my hand into his chest.

Tilting his head, he sits in the lounge chair in the corner of the room. I march toward him, grabbing my purse on the way before straddling his lap. Taking a moment to adjust myself on him, I rub the hardness against my panties. I begin grinding on him in slow circles, my hands around his shoulders.

"Don't move."

"So pushy," he says.

"Shut up." I pull myself closer to his body for better leverage, increasing the friction against his erection. "When I'm done, you will take your things and go. You will watch me from a distance because you are crowding my style and getting in the way of my trip. Do you understand?"

"I do not..."

"Don't argue with me. Just follow my orders." I feel the blade in my hand and smile. Leaning closer to him, I place the edge against his neck and press until I see blood.

"Do it." His voice trembles as a small trickle of blood runs through his beard.

I do my best to fight the swirling urges in my head and try to concentrate on the pleasure I feel. My hand will not release the knife, so I begin moving against him once more even as I press the blade deeper into his skin. He lets out a grunt that I understand to be pleasure, which makes me increase the tempo of my movements. Sweat gathers at my temples as I pant with effort, gripping his shoulders. Whimpering sounds begin to escape my lips as I feel my orgasm getting closer. Hair sticks to my face as I clutch against him. Waves of energy pulsate over my body, and I collapse in his arms.

He tries to push me off, but I cling to him with my arms around his neck. "Wait. You will hold me."

I continue to pant and sweat in his arms while his heavy breathing fills the vacuum of the room. He radiates warmth, and I don't want to end the embrace. With a sigh, I pull myself off his lap, place the knife on the nightstand and find my cigarettes. I sit at the desk and smoke. Ready to begin writing, I rip out the page of my notebook with his mark and wipe his blood off my hands with it before throwing it at him.

"I don't think you will, sir."

"What's that?" He appears perplexed.

I take a deep drag and exhale in his direction. "Be taking me to the museum. I can find my own fucking way. Now, get out."

Walking toward the door, he keeps his eyes on me while pulling at his beard. "I knew you wouldn't do it."

I wait for him to leave with a pen ready to make notes. Before I take my journey for the day, I scratch the following sentence on the page and sit back to contemplate.

Now that he asks, can I answer? What am I?

CONCEPTION

The taxi takes me to city's edge and drops me off a few hundred yards from Lake Erie. In front of me, there are oddly shaped buildings and a pyramid of glass and metal that's surrounded by castle type appointments. They almost look like guardhouses. Pausing at the curb in the crisp afternoon air, I try to take in the view, shielding my eyes from the sunlight reflecting off the water. A homeless man makes himself known to me, holding out a sign so tattered that I can't read the words.

"Please. Can you spare a dollar?"

I look into his eyes, and without thinking, pull a hundred dollar bill out of my purse. "Can you make change?"

His eyes widen in confusion at the sight of the bill. Chuckling, I press the bill into his filthy hand and watch him scurry away without so much as a thank you. Oh, the homeless today have no manners!

Walking towards the entrance, I spot the ticketing booth and stand behind a middle-aged couple holding hands. I wonder how long they have been together, so I try to solve the riddle by eavesdropping, but I can't decipher their whispers above the music, a rock song I'm not familiar with.

The line doesn't appear to be moving, causing me to slip into my thoughts. While wondering where Mr. Brown might be, I'm also forced to shoo away a memory of my father. An announcement over the speaker explains that a new exhibit will open at the month's end. A snapshot of that evening he bought me the shoes solidifies in my mind.

He drank a lot at the bar that afternoon...more than usual. His mood got darker with each hour, and his stare scared me more as dusk fell outside. He swerved the car toward home with one hand squeezing mine. I felt as if something awful might happen and began counting the time until he might pass out, going so far as to pour him a double whiskey to help that journey.

I pretended I was watching TV, but he only watched me with his red, angry eyes. He slurped whiskey, spilling much of it on his plaid shirt. When he stood up and staggered into the wall, I rushed to prop him up before he knocked over the TV and stereo.

"Let's go to bed, Daddy." I sighed and put his arm over my shoulder before leading him down the hall.

He mumbled and pawed at me. His hot breath tickled my neck, causing me to shiver. I crawled into bed and wrapped his arms around me, hoping he might fall asleep...

Screams snap me from my daydream, and I see people running in every direction but mostly toward the exits. Gunshots ring out and I feel a bullet graze my jacket moments before the man in front of me falls, blood spurting from his neck. I scan the room, but the chaos makes it impossible to locate the shooter. More shots ring out, giving me a better idea of the location. It feels like less than fifty feet.

The movie is still playing while I stand frozen. A worker catches a bullet as she tries to flee the ticket counter, and her brain flies out in pieces behind her in slow motion. The lady nearest to me tends to her fallen companion while bullets keep striking the floor. I see a man with cropped hair in a sports parka holding a gun. For a second, he turns away from me and shoots down an elderly woman, who was limping toward the bathrooms.

The shooter faces me and shoots the woman at my feet before aiming the gun at my head. His brows scrunch in confusion, probably not understanding why I'm not running or even lifting my arms to shield myself. Sirens approach the building. The man takes a few steps in my direction and checks the area, but it seems we're the last two left in the room. Hazel eyes lock on mine for what seems an eternity, but in reality, it's only mere seconds.

"Are you crazy?" he mumbles.

"I don't think so."

Maybe I am, but I don't feel any fear. Hand on my bag, I unzip the purse and grab my knife. His thumb flicks out, presses a button, and the magazine ejects on the floor before he jams another one into the open space. I back away with my heels slipping on the blood-soaked floor. I grab the ticket counter for support.

"There is something different about you." He comes closer, tilting his head. His breathing is heavy, causing the gun to rise and fall with the movements of his chest.

I know.

The scene plays out as if time has stopped. His eyes are calm, but my focus is on his finger stroking the trigger. He could fire; my death is chambered in his weapon. I have a fleeting thought of Ray and the smallest feeling of regret of not seeing him again. I dare to take another step away from the man. Will it all end right now? I guess I won't make it to Las Vegas after all.

Time starts again. I want to tell him that he'd be dead already if I had a gun, but there isn't much sense in saying it. I'll just close my eyes and wait for him to act. I just don't understand why he killed these random people but seems torn about what to do with me.

Just then, he turns from me, raising the gun and firing. My feet move, and my arm goes up. The distance between us vanishes while he continues to fire. The clip jams, and he stops to re-load a new cartridge. It allows me just enough time to drive the blade into his neck. He flails and falls, blood spraying in the air in all directions.

When I step away from his death torrent, the police spill into the room in force. A massive FBI agent tackles me, presses my face into the floor, and cuffs my hands in an instant.

As suddenly as it began, the episode is over, and the dead shooter lies several feet from me. The agent lifts me and leads me toward the front entrance. A reporter and a cameraman stand nearby. When I'm led outside, the reporter runs toward me with a microphone pointing into my face.

"Can you tell me what happened?" the reporter rushes his words.

"No."

"Is there anything you can tell us?" Her eyes scans me.

I look directly into the camera. "Hello world."

ENLIGHTENMENT

Vivaldi plays as I struggle to regain consciousness. This room is foreign to me with candles providing a bleak light in a heavy darkness that brings cold against my skin. Water drips in a constant beat all around me, but I can't see the source. I sit up on a black leather couch, and the panic spreads in my veins as I hear the faint sound.

"Where am I?" I manage to speak.

A low, quiet laugh answers me. Although I recognize the voice, I can't pinpoint the direction. The laugh grows closer, and someone steps into the candlelight. I see Father, naked with bloodstains on his neck, approaching me. His torso is covered in stab wounds, but he smiles at me.

"Somewhere in the afterlife," he says without a hint of emotion.

He sits next to me on the couch. The wounds seep blood and pus, causing me to recoil from the stench. Moving away from him proves impossible because he's suddenly on both sides of me.

"Leave me alone, Father. That time is over."

Laughing, he grabs a pipe out of the air and leans against the cushions. "It will never end," he thunders.

His hand leaves a bloody print on my leg. I scream, but no sound escapes my lips. The walls seem to shift as the music blares into my ears, mixing with my father's creeping stare.

When I try to rise to my feet, he laughs once again. "Wake up, little girl, they will be coming now."

***

Smoke reaches my nose before I open my eyes. Mr. Brown is sitting in a chair, holding a cigarette. I shudder and feel a wave of pain ripple down my limbs. *Of course.* I see him and not Ray. Closing my eyes, I hear him stand, the coins jingling in his pockets.

"You can't smoke in here."

"What are they going to do, arrest me?"

"Stay away from me. I remember you now," I say.

He grabs my purse from the tray stand to my right and begins rummaging through the contents. He takes the knife in his hand, rubbing his fingers over the smooth handle. A smile lifts his beard.

"And now we know the other one knows." He puts the knife in his pocket.

"Put that back."

"Ella, it's for your protection. You will be questioned now. Do I need to spell out the implications, or do we understand each other?"

"Is this where your teaching begins, Master Yoda?"

"Mentors are for writing. The type of thing you're suggesting only happens on TV shows for lemmings."

"I like TV shows, especially this one about a detective from Miami..."

"Be quiet."

I try to sit, but the pain sparking fire in my brain stops the attempt. "I will not listen to you, bully."

"I know you don't understand right now, but I'm trying to help you. After the mess you left in New York, that proposition became much more difficult. Now please, shut up and listen to me."

With a sigh, I cross my arms and wait for him to speak.

"They are almost here. You must tell them nothing. Do you understand? Don't admit to a thing even if they claim to possess evidence. Let them arrest you. Ray can buy a team of lawyers to battle them in court." He reaches out a hand and covers my eyes. "Wake up, Ella."

***

"Ella?"

I hear a voice, but my eyes won't open. I feel as if I'm trapped under ice, trying to break through to the surface and fighting toward the voice. When I wake up, I find myself in an empty, white room with some men surrounding the bed. The two closest to me seems like FBI agents. My vision remains blurry, and I struggle to clear my mind to focus. *Was I drugged?*

"There are some men here to ask you a few questions. Do you feel up to speaking with them?" the man who tackled me asks.

I can't focus on his face and look over his shoulder to see a man with dark skin and black hair looking at me. "Sure." The air seems to shake as I blink rapidly to steady my vision.

The man leaves me with two men: the dark one and a tall man with curly brown hair.

"Hello, gentlemen," I say.

"We've been waiting to speak to you for some time. You've been asleep for almost two days," the man with greased, black hair says to me with a low and soothing voice.

"Two days? I can't remember. What happened to me?"

"You killed a madman. It was a massacre. Six dead, including the shooter."

"A madman, you say. I guess I'm lucky to be alive."

"That's what we want to ask you. What did the man say to you before you stabbed him?"

"I don't recall him saying anything to me. He stared at me for a few seconds, and I think he was trying to shoot me then."

The dark man sits in the chair next to the bed, his head forming three targets for me to look at. Smoothing his tie against his chest, he pulls at his leather jacket. "We see his lips moving on the video recording. He spoke to you. We were hoping you'd be able to tell us what he said."

"Wait. Who are you?" I'm still trying to focus but only can make out his dark hair and skin.

"I'm with the FBI, Ella."

FBI? I can't imagine why he's questioning me now when my mind can't even process anything. It must be something of importance, but all I did was kill that shooter.

"Ella?"

"Yes?"

"You said some curious things in the ride downtown. Do you remember?"

Yes, I do remember, but that's none of your business, Mr. FBI man.

"No, I do not."

Pulling a small pad out of his jacket pocket, he flips the pages. Clearing his voice, he begins to read from his notes.

"...after being led outside, a reporter asked two questions. You looked into the camera and said hello, world..."

I stare at him. Nothing comes to mind.

"Ella? What did you mean by that?"

"I have no idea, sir."

"No need for formality. Call me Marcus."

"If you say so." It's still difficult to keep my eyes open.

Rubbing his chin, he glances at his notes, studying the words for some time. "Can you tell me what happened in New York?"

New York? What about New York?

"I can't remember what happened."

"Which part? The man you visited, or how he ended up dead?"

The reality that he *knows* cuts through the pain and clouds my mind. "I don't remember being in his place. He took me to meet friends, and we ate dinner. That's all."

Without speaking, Marcus begins placing pictures on the table next to my bed of the bloody carnage left at the Robert's house. I want to scream that I couldn't have done this thing, but I see stab wounds in Robert's body. *I didn't do this. I couldn't have.*

"Or perhaps you recognize these photos." This time, he lays out pictures of the boy I killed at the party.

I'm speechless, feeling weakness rushing over my body. My mind begins slipping back into the darkness and sliding down the passage into the black. "Marcus—" I begin to say as I fade into unconsciousness.

***

"Let me at least give her water. Is it really necessary to question her right this minute?" I hear the first man ask Marcus, but can't move my head, which is swimming in a sea of stars and waves.

"I'll see she gets water. Please go play nurse in another room," Marcus says, waiting for the nurse to leave.

The other agent leaves too and I'm left alone with Marcus. Taking a seat on the side of my bed, he brings the water bottle toward me and put the straw to my lips. The water cools my mouth, and some of the fog begins to clear.

"Thank you." I clear my throat.

He nods and places a small cassette recorder on the food tray next to the bed.

"What's that for?"

"A surprise. I've been waiting quite some time to play this tape for you." With a clicking of a button, the tape starts to play.

...(phone ringing)
...911, What is the emergency?"
...(long pause)...I killed my father.
...What is your name?

...(a pause of a minute)...Ella Thomas

He didn't even wait for me to wake up to spring the trap. In my state, I can't understand him rushing like an amateur. At least get me something to eat. This man knows nothing about women.

"Tell me what happened."

"You know already if you found this tape."

"Yes, but I want to hear it from you."

My throat hurts, and I motion for more water. He does and watches me drink greedily.

"You will never hear that story from me."

He walks out of the room and returns with a tablet computer in his hands.

"I've read your stories. Your novel interests me. In it, you talk about everything except what happened that day. You mentioned it once and never returned to it again."

"What happened doesn't concern you."

Tapping at the computer screen, he jumps from the file with my novel to pictures of Robert. "I think it does." Placing the tablet in my hand, he takes a seat at the far end of the bed.

I scroll through the pictures. "Arrest me or not. I have nothing to say."

"I don't want to arrest you, Ella. My partner wants that outcome, but I do not. I simply want to know how Ray fits in all this. Why did he leave Holden Farms to you?"

I keep tapping at the screen in silence.

He produces several sheets of filler paper stapled together from his jacket pocket. Placing the packet on the table, he points at the title.

July 13th

"Do you want to tell me now?"

Where did he find this? I thought he gave me the lost stories in NYC. Turning the page, I see large bubble style cursive.

Today is my birthday. I am thirteen on the thirteenth of July, 2004. What am I doing for my special day? I'm having my father killed. Yes, you read it right. I mean it. Today, my father will die.

"This is a story," I say, reading on.

"A story that happened. You did kill your father."

"You don't understand—"

"Make me understand." He brings his hand down on the chair with sudden force.

"I killed my father, but that story is fiction. It didn't happen that way," I plead, trying to lean forward to see him better.

Waves of pain return, forcing me to rest my head against the pillow again. I close my eyes.

His shoes clicks on the floor, and the sound gets closer.

"Did you kill your father because of Ray?"

He seems to know everything. What does he want?

"I killed my father because..." I can't continue.

He takes another look at the file and stands. "Ella, you've killed three men the same way. Are you aware that classifies you as serial killer?"

I am aware it classifies me as one, yes. But...am I?

I don't want to answer the question. The question proves too much. I can't fight the darkness from taking over and take me deep into an abyss.

ESCAPE

The sound of rustling papers wakes me up. Mr. Brown is stuffing things into my backpack with an outfit thrown on the chair, which I assume is for me. My head isn't throbbing like before. How long did I sleep this time, and where did the agents go? He looks over and motions for me to get out of bed. There's no dizziness as I swing my legs over the side and put my feet on the floor.

"Get dressed," he barks, opening a map on the table.

"Nice to see you too, grumpy pants. You could at least ask how I'm feeling."

He watches as I pull off my hospital gown and put on the jeans and sweatshirt he set out for me. I smile at him, trying to keep my eyes on his.

"We have no time for that. They will return and you need to be gone." He taps a finger on the map, showing a route he highlighted. It runs through Chicago and Omaha before landing on Denver.

"I'm not going that way." I shake my head, not understanding the map.

"Exactly. You will leave this map here, and it will buy us time. With luck they will watch those roads as well as the ones to the south. You can escape into the southern states undetected. By that time, Ray's lawyers will find cover for you, providing you don't commit any further acts of stupidity. Can you behave, or do I need to chain you to a bed?"

I resist the opportunity to make a joke. His eyes do not show any mirth, so I settle on a mere nod as answer. The map details stops and even hotel reservations, which undoubtedly Mr. Brown took the time to research and book. It's too bad, though. I wanted to see Chicago and Denver. Perhaps I'll get to see those cities another time on another trip. The thought of fleeing south and missing out on many places on my list fills me with sadness, but it's better than spending another moment with the FBI. I don't even remember the name of the man who was wearing the leather jacket.

"Tell me where I'm supposed to go."

"Go south through Ohio, keep off the major roads, and head toward Indianapolis. Please try to be discreet." He grabs a baseball cap from the bag and places it roughly over my ears. "And stop looking so damned pretty. Don't be in a rush to get anywhere. Keep away from the big cities for now."

Looking in the mirror, I arrange my hair under the cap to make myself look presentable. "Where will you be?"

"Checking you into the hotels on the map we will leave for them."

I look at him in the mirror, hoping he might explain further. Shaking his head in disgust, he lifts my arm and slides the backpack over my shoulders.

"You don't want to know."

My eyes go wide as I figure out his meaning. "You're going to find a girl that—"

Pressing a finger to my lips, he grunts. "Don't speak another word."

"Okay." I stick my tongue out at him.

Ignoring me, he launches into instructions. "In the convenience store parking lot across the street, you'll find a blue Ford Escort with the keys under the visor. All your things are in the trunk. The car doesn't look like much, but I assure you it runs well. All the levels are checked, the tank is full, and you need do no more than get in and drive south. Can you manage that?"

"When will I see you again?"

"If all goes right, Las Vegas. You will proceed to Dallas and meet Ray there on Valentine's Day at Hotel..."

"What?"

He closes his eyes just as he turns away from me. If I didn't know better, I think he might cry.

"I don't know what else to say. Will I be able to call you or text?"

"Do not call that number for anything less than an emergency."

"What...?"

"We are out of time. You must leave at once."

Dragging me by the arm, he leads me down the hall and through an emergency exit as a group of men approach the room.

"Follow the hall all the way to the back entrance. Don't walk directly to the convenience store. They'll be watching the street. Walk two blocks, cross over, and double back. Don't waste time, but don't run."

Without another word, he vanishes into a side door. I make my way down the service hallway, taking the back entrance. After I scan the parking lot for any sign of agents, I move toward the road and head in the opposite direction of the store as instructed.

As I wait at the crosswalk, I can't help but feel excited about this adventure. It's like something out of a movie. I will miss my car, though. Having to trade a GM for a Ford hurts me somewhere inside, but I push the thought away. Crossing the street, I walk as quickly as my legs allow without running to the store. The Escort is parked near the bathrooms and out of sight of the main road. He thought of everything.

When I open the door, I see a duffle back on the floor of the passenger seat. I start the car and adjust the mirrors before unzipping the bag to inspect the contents. There are stacks of cash, new nondescript clothing, and a cell phone. A note falls to the floor, and I pick it up.

After you leave the city, throw your cellphone into the woods. Do not turn on the new one unless you have dire need. Stay off the main roads. Avoid all the major cities of Ohio as those will be watched. If you need to contact me for any reason, you will find an email address stored in the phone. Use that and not the number. Do NOT call for any reason. Good luck, Ella.

Without wasting any time, I take RT-77 south out of the city, turning off the main highway. I plan on circling 77 until I reach RT-70, which I will follow to Indianapolis, making sure to exit and avoid all major cities as he told me. In a way, I will miss Mr. Brown even though I told him to leave less than a week ago. This trip seems far different than it did back in Utica and NYC. There's no point in looking back. I must go to Dallas. I don't even know if I'll see Ray there or if Mr. Brown told me that to get me moving.

No matter. I ride toward Indianapolis. The journey continues.

***

When I arrive at Indianapolis, I've already grown tired of dusty one-stop-light towns with coffee shops full of stale old men. There are no words to capture my state of mind since Cleveland. I have yet to come to grips with that day. Thoughts of the shooting, the FBI, and Mr. Brown swirl around but never form a coherent picture. I failed to add anything to my narrative, spending most of my time reading Austen and Dickens to occupy my mind.

But I can't take it any longer. Having to hide for the past week and avoiding cities makes me crave the company of men my own age. I feel the beginnings of excitement in my veins as I dress in my hotel room. After doing my hair and makeup, I put on a skin-tight purple dress with gold trim that shows plenty of pale leg. I'm sure to attract eyes and hands of desire.

I search for a bar, a happening bar that guarantees some action. It doesn't take long to spot a building with black sheer façade with a long line of people. Finding a place to park, I check my face in the rearview mirror and grab my gray purse, which match my gray pumps. I stride by the line, confident that my hip-hugging dress will gain me access.

The bouncer, a rather large man with tatted arms and neck, gropes me with his eyes and ushers me inside. From the pounding of the bass deep inside my chest as I enter the bar, I know tonight will be different from the recent nights I wasted with old men. College boys in a circle pack the center of the room. I smile.

Swaying with the music to an open spot, I slide onto the stool and nod to the bartender for attention. He looks around mid-twenties, a college type with close-clipped goatee and a tight-fitting black uniform. Brown eyes wait upon me, and I resist the urge to order a whiskey. I'm going to be a girl tonight.

"I'll take a cosmopolitan." I lock eyes with him, praying somehow he doesn't check my ID. Without a word, he busies himself with my drink. *Whew.* I start to scour the room for candidates, hoping to see just the right boy whom I'll allow to take me wherever college boys take their girls. The drink appears at my hand without my notice. I run a finger along the rim and lick my finger for effect. I hope some boy is watching me because I want to set the lure deep and snug in some boy's cheek.

I cross my legs and let a foot move with the music. A gray pump slips off my foot, and I instantly look around to see if anyone has noticed. One boy with a university cap and blue sweatshirt eyes me. At the same time, a man older than the boys filling the room appears at my side and kneels next to me. His arm brushes my leg as he picks my shoe off the ground.

Fighting the urge to gasp, I glance into his pretty hazel eyes. Hints of wrinkles form around his eyes while he smiles up at me.

"May I?" he asks.

I assume that's what he said since I can't hear the words over the thumping of the bass. I nod, and he takes my foot in his hand. It feels both rough and lovely against my skin. He slides the shoe over my toes, his fingers caressing my ankles.

The guy sitting next to me rises and yields his seat to the man without a word. The man sits and orders a drink with a flick of his wrist. His gaze returns to me after the bartender whisks his drink to him.

"Cheers." He lifts his drink to mine with his hazel eyes transfixed on me. Sipping on his beer, he turns the stool to face me. "You're different."

"Is that a line?"

"No, it's an observation. You have very pretty calves. That is a line." He grins.

"Thank you, sir," I whisper.

A crowd of college boys push against the bar, forcing the man to inch his stool closer to mine.

Smelling his pine scented cologne, I let the music sweep over me. "How am I different?"

"For one, you haven't sipped your drink. Usually, the people your age are working on drink three after twenty minutes."

"Go on," I say.

"Also, you're looking around, but not as if you're waiting for someone. You look as if you're casting a net and waiting to see who'll be your victim."

His assessment startles me and I take a large sip of my drink to settle my nerves. "I'm looking for something to happen. No victims here."

Still grinning, he lapses into silence. But his intense gaze doesn't stop, and his palm moves to rest against my knee.

As I listen to the beats, my eyes scan the room. I feel his hand gliding along my skin and creeping under my dress. The squeezing of my thigh sends me gasping and almost makes me spill my drink. He hand spins me and notices my empty glass. He smiles and signals for another while keeping his hand against my inner thigh. A finger swirls in circles, coming closer to my panties with each movement. I let my eyes close, waiting for him to do as he wishes.

A gentle tap on my arm lets me know that my new drink has arrived. Once again, he holds out his own glass. After clinking glasses, I take a sip, not forgetting my courtesies on this occasion.

"Tell me your story," he says with a casual air, but his eyes maintain the same intensity.

"I'm off to Vegas to see about a boy," I respond, but the volume of the music disperses my attempt at humor into a thin wisp.

"And this?" He points at the room with a sweep of his arm while his fingers find a soft spot to caress.

"Oh," I moan against my will.

Instead of stopping, he leans closer, pressing his cheek against mine. "Shall we go?" he whispers the words into my ear, his thick fingers still caressing me.

My voice fails, and I grab my purse from the bar. I walk straight toward the exit, turning only to make sure he's following. He's just within an arm's reach behind me, and when I turn, he grabs me and pulls me into an embrace. The kiss is slow, melting me into a silent scream. I want so desperately for him to taste all of me now right here at the bar.

With the end of our kiss, we walk to my car, holding hands. The roughness of his palm keeps me from floating into the night. Parting long enough for me to open the door and start the engine, he kisses me again before I begin the drive to the hotel. His hands find my bare legs, rubbing and squeezing them. The distraction nearly causes a crash as I make a left into the hotel parking lot. When I park in the first space available, he's all over me in a rush, ripping at my dress. My breasts are exposed without a fight, but I manage to push him off me.

"No," I pant, pulling the dress back in place and turning off the engine.

He exhales as we exit the car and we make it to my hotel room. Just as the door closes, he pins me against the wall, and my cheek becomes pressed against the mirror. My purse falls to the floor. Talk is no use as he bites my neck and hikes my skirt. I gasp once again. I hear his zipper opening, and instantly, I feel him slam into me, taking my breath away as my body hits the wall.

Gripping my hair, he takes me in hurried, frenzied thrusts. I can't say if I'm protesting, moaning, or screaming, but I feel hot and wet as he mumbles into my ear. My legs buckle as he holds me up. One of his hands grip my hair, and the other is holds my waist. He continues to pound me with lightning quick strokes as I leave lipstick marks on the mirror. Lifting me higher and leaning me back against the dresser, he uses my own weight to impale me. His arms manipulate my body with force, and I feel helpless against his assault.

He throws me onto the bed. My stomach is pushed down into the comforter with him still inside me. With his hand firmly gripping my hair, he pulls me and thrashes against me with such force a wave of faintness passes over me. I feel him begin to climax inside me and hold the bed as he grunts and seeds me.

Eyeing my purse, I feel a desire to reach for it but manage to push the thought from my mind. The moment is gone. The storm is over, and he collapses on top of me with his sweat dripping on my back and down my neck. I feel his arms wrap around me, and I let the corners of sleep descend over my consciousness.

I wake up later, alone and cold. Shaking off sleep, I walk naked into the bathroom and run the water. I step into the shower and lean my head against the wall. Letting the water run over me, I play the night's events in my mind. I can't say it happened the way I expected, nor can I say the reason I didn't grab my purse. But I remember one thing. Tomorrow, I will be a new city. St. Louis.

ST. LOUIS

A thick, dirty slush coats my boots as I walk toward the entrance of the gas station on the outskirts of the city. The last two days of constant snow made travel difficult. I have to spend a day here to let the storm pass rather than forcing my way south through roads, which will be clogged with plows and other traffic. Paying the clerk, I glance up to the arch that seems to be dominating the midafternoon winter sky almost like an entrance to the city.

It feels as if I'm being watched. When I follow the stares, I realize it's due to my skirt flapping in the wind, showing bits of thighs and bare knees. My gaze falls on an older gentleman and I shrug. Mind your own business. Does everyone really need to stare? I can't be the only woman wearing a skirt today. It's not freezing outside. Well, technically perhaps, but it's my preference.

Returning to my car, I drive the streets in search of a place to get lunch. I'm starving and feel the rumbling in my belly. Searching for diners on my phone, I set course for the first one on the list called City Diner. It looks upscale and trendy with red-stained wood framing the windows and neon lights penetrating the gloom of winter. Entering, I wait to be seated. The hostess shakes her head when I tell her I will be dining alone. Sue me.

I place my writing materials out on the table over the paper menus. A waitress comes over to my table and seems to expect me to order something without even giving me the required fake greeting. Tall and gangly with brown hair in a ponytail, she taps a pen against a notepad, displaying her obvious irritation. With a sigh, I push my tablet to the side and look at the menu.

"Coffee, Coke, water, sirloin—rare—with fries," I say in rapid fire.

"Thank you," she says with a smile and a wink.

Making a few notes in my journal, I drift off into a daydream and don't notice the steaming cup of coffee along with soda and water. That was fast. A raw winter day like today reminds me of the one from my past. A day that brought great change to my life.

School was let out early that day due to the snow. I trudged through slush and sleet up the hill toward home, getting covered from head to toe as cars zoomed by and sprayed me with a mix of sand and salt.

As soon as I got home, I headed for the shower to wash off the grit. I neither heard nor saw Father, but he most certainly saw me. I started the water, and he touched me on the shoulder, which made me jump and scream.

"Miss? Can you cut into your steak to see if it's cooked the way you want please?" The waitress says.

Jolted out of my daydream, I pick up a knife and fork and cut into the meat. "Sorry, just thinking about something."

She looks at my writing supplies and back up at me. "What are you writing?"

Peeking at the middle, I see the steak is indeed rare. I smile. There are few things in life worse than an overcooked steak. "I'm making notes for a novel."

"Oh?" Her eyebrows lifts. "What's it about?"

"Driving cross country to see about a boy I once knew from my childhood that I hope will be my future husband."

"Sounds romantic." She giggles, twirling hair with a pen.

"I think of it as a kind of romantic fantasy."

She pauses and thinks on a response before speaking. "You seem too young to say once knew about a boy you mean to marry now. How old are you?"

"I'm twenty."

"This sounds like one of those childhood romances. I bet the boy was a classmate, probably sat in front of you in homeroom or took the same bus to school. Am I right?"

"No, he worked as a clerk in a convenience store near my house," I say.

"Wait a minute. How old were you and the boy?"

"I met him a few days before I turned thirteen, and he was no boy. He was thirty-four, I believe."

Her eyes narrow, and she shakes her head in disbelief. "That's not a romance, you know. There's a name for that. It's called child abuse."

"It's my story." I close the notebook from her prying eyes.

"Enjoy your steak," she mutters with disgust before walking back to the kitchen.

I will.

The fries are too salty for my taste, but the steak is seasoned with garlic and butter, my favorite. I savor every bite, trying to shake off the nasty conversation. Soon, my thoughts return to father and that day. In my mind, I can picture the bathroom with the matching, faded-pink towels Mother used to love so much and the flower print shower curtain. Oh, mother.

On that day, I immediately knew something was different because he seemed quite sober yet began to undress without a word with his red, angry eyes on me. Drunk and mad make a bad combination, but nothing can be worse than anger in the middle of the day. Trying to ignore him, I jumped in the shower as if he weren't. My arms began to shake as I tried to wash myself and nearly fainted when he pushed the shower curtain aside and stepped into the tub.

"Can I get you anything else?"

I look up to see her standing a few feet from me. The diner seems to be emptying, and the waitress is in no hurry to move along. I close my notebook and lean back in the chair. I light a cigarette and study her, wondering what she wants.

"I would love a slice of pie with ice cream."

She sighs and rushes off to fill the order. The thought crosses my mind that I might be her last table. She wants me to pay out. Oh well, I want pie.

Besides, I'm not leaving until I get this chapter finished. I need to say what I have to say. Returning quickly with the pie and a coffee pot, she refills my cup before sliding my check onto the table.

"Am I keeping you from anything important?"

She bites her lip and looks around. "Not really, but waiting for one last table to pay kinda sucks. Please don't tell anyone I said that."

Pulling a hundred dollar bill from the table, I push it towards her. "I think this will make up for your trouble, no?"

She gasps but grabs it and disappears into the kitchen once again.

Smoking in silence, I watch the few remaining customers begin to clear out. A group of old men make a racket arguing about the big football game of February 5th. Could these men be more typical? The game is over. There's nothing more to argue about, boys. The score is recorded. *Move on!* Back to my notes.

I gripped the knob for balance as Father did what he had been waiting for months to do. The sudden pain caused me to lurch forward, turning the knob in the process that brought a cascade of hot water on him.

"God damn it, Ella, hold still for Christ's sake," he yelped in anger.

"Sorry, Father," I managed to say, turning the knob back. A red fire of growing pain filled my belly as his fingers gripped my sides. I just wanted the moment to be over...

"What are you writing about now? Why do you switch from the tablet to the notebook?" She sits across from me with a cup of coffee in front of her.

Join me, why don't you?

"It's all from the same story, but I like to keep things separate. Right now, I'm writing about the time I lost my virginity."

The lady smiles and seems to fall into her daydream. I can only assume that she's thinking about her first time. Smiling, she bites her lip again. It's obvious that she's itching to talk.

Shaking my head, I oblige her. "Who took your virginity?"

"My first boyfriend. It was after the spring dance in an old Buick outside the city. I remember it like it was yesterday." Her eyes gloss with emotion as she continues to sift through the details. "What about you? Who was your first?"

I place another hundred on the check and pack my things. Putting the backpack over my shoulder, I stand and turn toward her one last time. "My father."

OKLAHOMA CITY

Only after I tell the waitress of *that* day, I feel cramping in my midsection. I waste no time and stop at a convenience store to buy a box of tampons and several chocolate bars. A girl can never have too much chocolate, no matter what men think. Between remembering the day I lost my virginity and getting my period, I decide not to spend the night in St. Louis and head toward Oklahoma City.

My mood grows darker as I drive into the storm, chewing the candies mindlessly. The memories of my father and those months before Ray came into my life fill my head. *Lovers.* That word resurfaces most often, and I can't deny its accuracy. I shake my head as I picture that day at Applebee's. Thinking of it makes it difficult to drive, so I stop at a rest area for a much-needed nap. Darkness grips the sky as I recline the seat. Pulling a ball cap over my eyes, I lock the doors.

It hurts to think of how I pushed Father to take me on a date. For weeks, I pressured, nagged, and begged him. Eventually, it boiled down to plain blackmail, the basic gist being only a dinner out on the town could guarantee my continued silence. He finally caved in to my relentless demands and told me that we would go out next Saturday like a regular couple.

I don't know why I can't shake this memory. It seems to flash into my mind more than any other. I can recall seeing myself dressing carefully in front of the long mirror, taking extra time brushing my hair to a perfect shine. Putting on the heels he bought me, I practiced walking in the kitchen as I waited for him to be ready. I watched him with growing impatience while he slugged beer down on the recliner.

Finally, he shut off the television, and I followed him in silence to the car. I was so excited that I didn't want to do anything to put him in a bad mood. And since he started drinking early, that could happen quite easily. Stealing constant glimpses of him during the ride, I didn't notice bypassing our usual dinner spots and taking the highway toward Worcester.

"Where are we, Daddy?"

"Applebee's, just as you wanted."

"This isn't our Applebee's."

Pulling me aside before entering, he gripped my upper arm, squeezing hard for a moment. "Don't play stupid. Cut the shit right here and now."

Nodding, I kept my eyes on his, trying to smile nicely for him. Grunting, he dragged me inside. We were led to a booth by a teenage hostess wearing large hoop earrings. Father plopped down onto the cushion as the girl placed menus on the table. When she turned her back, I scooted closer to him, ignoring his groans of protest and feeble attempts to push me away. I knew he wouldn't cause a scene and would relent if I refused to move unless forced.

I cringed when Father ordered a whiskey because I knew the situation could get ugly in short order if he got drunk. As she left, I slipped my hand into his, hoping to calm him. He stroked my palm with his thumb and exhaled as I inched closer to him, pressing my leg against rough denim.

"Be careful. People are watching."

"Oh, Daddy, let them watch. We are lovers, after all."

Sucking in air, his body tensed against me before he took a gulp of whiskey. "Don't say that," he whispered to me through a clenched jaw.

His fingertips turned white, gripping the glass. I leaned my head on his shoulder and waited for his anger to pass, stroking the back of his hand with my fingertips.

"Don't worry, Daddy, I won't ever tell anyone."

A loud noise snaps my daydream, and I bolt upright in the seat to see a group of boys chasing each other in the parking lot. The clock tells me I've been napping for almost two hours. I return my seat to its original position before putting the car into gear. Moments after I'm on the interstate, I see signs indicating that I'm less than an hour from Oklahoma City. I want sleep and to push these thoughts from my mind.

Flipping on the stereo, I light a cigarette and sift through the remnants of the memory of that day. It seems to stand out because of my promise. Some, of course, will scream and holler about the insanity of the situation, but I didn't see it that way. I enjoyed being out to dinner on my father's arm. I felt like an adult. I mattered. I never felt more loved than sitting there holding his hand and leaning on his arm inside that busy restaurant.

Crushing the cigarette in the ashtray, I look up at the skyline of the city in the distance before tapping the number of the hotel that was programmed into my phone to confirm my reservation. I hope I don't get a hassle at this late hour. To my surprise, all is in order and I arrive at the Holiday Inn Express without any incident. Without wasting a second, I find the room and collapse on the bed. Sleep takes me within moments.

***

I wake from a dreamless sleep to a throbbing soreness in my legs. A small knot of tightness in my lower back makes me curl into a tight ball, keeping me in bed for a few more minutes. Stumbling to the kitchenette, I start a pot of coffee and turn on the TV. The financial channel. Of course, I prepare myself mentally for an all-day-marathon. There's so much to catch up before seeing Ray in a few days, and I haven't forgotten how much he wanted me to be informed in this subject.

Money seems to be his entire world these days, which doesn't resemble the man I knew as a child. Although I'm not sure how he came to all of his money, I assume it must have come from his father. On the other hand, the last I knew, his father cut him out of the will. I must ask him about it when I meet him in Dallas, but for now, I listen to a panel of people arguing about the latest news from the Federal Reserve meeting on monetary policy—whatever that means.

As I'm having my coffee and listen, I swear I can hear the rattling of coins like in a casino when I watch the constant scrawl of letters and numbers on the screen. Isn't Wall Street another form of gambling? Truth be told, I don't have a great grasp of the whole thing, but I'm sure once Ray explains it to me, I might change my mind. The screen displays the stock prices going up and down all day long. It really doesn't make any sense to me at this point.

Money indeed is a gray area for me. Like everyone else, I love shopping and fine dining, but I abhor the basic truth that comes with membership in this country. The only thing that matters about your existence as an American is your net worth.

I don't want my entire life to revolve around money. Writing, and in a more general way art and all things culture, hold the dearest spots of my heart and soul. I know it's a job, but how can this woman on the television talk about this all day long? Doesn't her soul bleed every time she squawks her immortal line about do you know where your money is?

Time for a break. Turning on my tablet, I read over the last few chapters of my story. I can feel the disgust of my readers and hope they will still read it. Then again, I can only write the truth regardless of how much I wish it were different.

The phone dings, alerting me of a new email. Excitement flows in my stomach when I see Ray's name on the screen.

Something has come up, and I will not be able to meet you in Dallas. I have made a reservation for you at the best hotel in the city and hope you will be able to find some enjoyment for yourself. I'm sorry to disappoint you, but I have important business matters that I must attend to. I will contact you as soon as I can.

Yours always,

Ray

It's almost as if he read my chapter and sent this email to demonstrate. Money comes before the woman he claims will be his next wife. Oh, how this vexes me. I want to shake him and ask what can be so important to break plans with me on Valentine's Day.

The lady begins a rant about yearly stock performance when I click off the television. Learning how to count my money can wait now that I'll be alone in Dallas. Mr. Brown would've been handy to have around right now, so he could get me some alcohol. I'll have to manage somehow since I need something stronger than cream in my coffee at this moment. I tune out everything and succumb to the silence of the room.

Sometimes, all you can say is...*men.*

DALLAS

The cramps continue as I drive south on I-35 toward Dallas. The early morning sky seems cold and empty. While I navigate through the thick traffic, the faint outlines of a city form in the distance. The skyline begins to appear, and impressive skyscrapers rise from the earth. This city seems massive. I keep to the middle lane, heading downtown in search of my hotel.

My mind is full of needs and wants for chocolate, a bath, and a million other things before the image of frozen yogurt locks into place. Thanks to my phone, I find one in less than ten minutes. The cute sign in pink and blue displays "iheartyogurt" with a heart in the logo.

Pulling my parka tight to my face and carrying my backpack, I step out into the cold stillness of the morning. I stomp my shoes a few times to shake the numbness from my legs. As I get inside, I regret that my craving isn't something warmer. It's no shock that the place is empty save for a middle aged man in the corner shuffling paperwork. Rubbing my hands together as I look at the menu, I know I'll order the Berry Bonanza, except for some reason, I continue to stare at it for some time. My brain is locked in a messy place again. Now, I can't seem to pull myself together enough to step to the counter and place my order.

"Miss?" A teenage girl with light brown hair stares at me over her thick-rimmed glasses.

I mouth my order and hand her some money without realizing how much it is or if I have change coming in return. Overcome with thoughts of Ray, I take my yogurt and sit in a booth. It tastes amazing but can't distract me from the simple truth — Ray broke his word to me. Again. Trying to brush that aside, I start to check my accounts and email on my tablet. There's another email from Ray.

I reserved a room for you at the Ritz Carlton. Treat yourself to a day of spa and shopping or whatever else you desire. Know that I wanted to be with you, but business makes that impossible. I am in the beginning stages of purchasing a casino and do not have the time to explain all the complexities. But know this. This shall be our future.

Until I see you, after all these years.
Ray

I don't know what to believe. His message only leaves me with more questions. Will I actually see him when I get to Vegas? Am I just being jerked around or avoided? What does he mean about a casino? That's his excuse? I don't have to accept it. I'll do exactly the same thing without him here that I planned for us together. All I want is a special dinner alone in the hotel room. Some things are best left simple.

The map application alerts me of the route to the Ritz Carlton, and as if on cue, I'm out of yogurt.

Bracing myself for the cold, I push outside to my car and backtrack on the directions to hit the Starbucks in desperate need of caffeine and warmth. Reversing course makes the female voice on the navigation chirp at me. When it stops, I use my phone to book a reservation for an early dinner at Fearing's Restaurant.

The building looks as if it belongs in NYC, not Texas, but I won't deny the charm of the tree-lined entrance that affords a view of Trinity River. Pain grips me and turns the dull process of registration into an unseemly task. I really don't want anyone looking at me because I didn't have time to do my makeup or my hair. Inside the bathroom, I stand in front of the mirror and am stunned at the face staring back at me.

The dark circles shade my blue eyes. Fatigue has done its job. I brush my hair before applying lipstick and eye makeup. I'm more careful with my appearance during the time of the month. I can't explain why. Anyway, I'm pretty certain I look better than I did a few minutes ago. My reservation isn't until this evening, so I walk into the bar area, hoping I might be able to buy an appetizer and con the bartender into giving me a cocktail.

Two men sit at opposite ends of the honey onyx stained wood bar, comprising the entirety of the clientele. Both eye me with what borders on hostility. I can't help smiling as their eyes gawk at my pink sweatpants. The bartender watches me without offering or asking me anything.

"Might I get a bite to eat and a drink if it wouldn't be any trouble?" I say, batting my eyelashes at him. I ignore the grumbling and biting pains in my abdomen.

He places a menu in front of me, and the salmon with apricot barbeque glaze catches my attention.

"ID."

"I left it in my room." I try to remain nonchalant.

With a sigh, the bartender crosses his arms and waits for me to order. "Are you really staying in the hotel or are you just meeting someone?"

I don't like his insinuation and slide my keycard on top of the counter.

He lets out a low whistle and leans toward me. "Are you really staying in the Ritz-Carlton suite?"

"Yes, really. Now please, may I have a Martini?" I point at a bottle of Kettle One and walk away from the bar to take a seat on a leather couch.

As I wait for my drink, I place my tablet and notebook on a cherry wood table. I ready myself to write, the bartender places the drink next to me on a coaster and walks away.

"Put that drink on my bill," the man from the other table says to the bartender.

Nausea passes through me when I get a clear look at his fleshy face and thick, coarse hair that is obviously combed over a bald spot.

"No," I say.

There is no need to get into it with this man. I don't want to hear his lines. I don't want to hear anything. A migraine starts to build up. Hearing his voice heighten the cramps and sharpens the pain ripping through my body.

"You're beautiful," he spews out the words.

Not acknowledging his existence, I finish my drink and signal the bartender for another.

Talk to me again and I'll slit your throat. A voice in my mind screams, and I wish to put all the pain and discomfort I feel into him via my knife. Of all the men to chat me up in a bar, I get stuck with a gramps wearing dentures that keep shifting in his mouth, making a clicking sound each time he takes a breath.

"Listen, not today. My boyfriend stranded me, I'm in a strange city, and it's that time of the month. Can you please leave me alone?"

"I didn't mean to bother you..." he stammers.

"What do you think, I'm going to give in to your charms and take you to my suite? You're old enough to be my grandfather." I frown.

"Age is just a number," he says, smiling at me.

I take a gulp from my new drink and clear my head. *Invite him to your room.* I spin round, but I see nobody except for the bartender, who is busy polishing glassware.

"Have dinner with me."

Letting out a growl, I slam my palm on the table. "I've only been here for five minutes, and already I have douchebag hitting on me. Can't I just have a fucking lunch without you bothering me?"

The man keeps grinning at me as if he doesn't understand my words.

"Do you hear me? I'm on my period. No sex."

He snorts and sips scotch, scanning my body. "You don't bleed *everywhere.*"

Did he really say that? My blood boils, and my face feels flush. *Invite him to your room.* The voice echoes over and over again. *He'll go as sweet as a lamb.* Now, I can't suppress a giggle.

"No, I don't think so, sir. Perhaps another time," I say with a wink before gathering my things.

This man isn't worth my time, and no matter how vulgar he talks, I can't justify inviting him to my room. I finish my drink and walk toward the bar, throwing a hundred dollar bill at the bartender.

"Keep the change."

***

A tremor travels down my leg as I ease into the claw-foot tub. The pain is sudden and intense. *Ow. Ow. That's hot.* Cramps grip my thighs, calves, and feet when the heat penetrates my skin. I lower my body until the water reaches my neck, and days of travel tension release from me. Even when I exhale and try to relax, I can't stop the flood of memories from invading my mind. Can I let go of all the anger and resentment filling my body? I feel like a pawn in Ray's game even though I set this journey in motion. How did it all spin out of control? From the moment Mr. Brown intruded, things went south.

Now, I'm in Dallas. Why am I here? I can't figure out whether I'm been duped or jilted. Perhaps, I'm just out in left field and have no idea what's going on right now. Why am I running around the country when I'm so close to Vegas? The novel progresses, and soon, I'll have a draft to show Ray, so there's no reason to delay. My plan of being in Vegas by summer will move up a few months.

The thought of Vegas and its comforting heat makes me relax. And I love a bath on those worst days of the month when everything seems to hurt and screams for a massage. Spending an hour submerged from life helps me concentrate. A spa day sounds grand because I can take time out for the simple pleasures and not let myself be so obsessed with writing or watching CNBC.

And what about my novel? I certainly have a mess on my hands and seem to lose the narrative altogether at times. I keep telling myself that this is my first attempt at a longer work that I need to finish at all costs. Then comes the revision. The task proves more difficult when the novel is a memoir. It's hard to remain objective when it's about my father. All I can do is tell it as I remember and let the readers decipher the message.

More than anything, a single question keeps flashing in my mind. What am I? I have killed, but I don't think that defines me as a killer. At least, that's not the way I perceive myself. I am a writer. The killing was incidental. Until I'm convicted and incarcerated, those deaths don't count. Actually, those memories are like movie clips that play in my mind on an endless reel, a constant loop of blood and death that I don't associate with me in any particular way.

I do recall the boy from that party long ago. That boy was the first...if I don't count Father. I wrote about it but skipped the murder scene. I left that part out of the story because it's unnecessary. Besides, the details get garbled in my mind, and the distinction between story and reality becomes unclear.

However, there is one count that I'm certain about. Ray isn't here in Dallas with me. This suite echoes with space, occupying almost 2,400 square feet. It makes the solitude more acute and almost impossible to enjoy this unabashed display of luxury. Champagne sits on ice, and the kitchen brims with a sampling of everything on the room service menu. But I don't have the desire to eat or drink. I wish for Ray to be here, holding me.

Valentine's Day being tomorrow doesn't improve my mood. Will he pass Valentine's Day in the company of another woman? A shudder passes over my skin...no that thought will not do. I can't dwell on things out of my control. I must get out of this room. Stepping out of the bath, I pull a robe over my shoulders and walk into the kitchen. Pouring myself a cup of coffee, I sit at the table and stare out the window into the afternoon winter sky.

VALENTINE'S DAY

I hate this day and everything it stands for, but I must do something tonight. I can't bah humbug today, can I? What will he think of me? It's bad enough the bartender is staring at me and dissecting me. I have moped around this bar for the last three days, trolling for men and waiting for Valentine's. Sipping a martini at three in the afternoon in an empty bar in my sweat pants makes him stare all the more.

"Another?" he asks.

The drink isn't empty, but I guess he can't think of anything else to say. Why doesn't he ask for my number for my phone or room? He's big in the shoulders, and I can imagine him without a shirt. I like that vision. When I glance at him, his eyes contain no mirth, and he doesn't seem playful.

"Make it a beer," I blurt out, pushing cigarette butts in circles around an ashtray. I use a match to make a pile of the ashes.

"What kind?" he asks, looking annoyed.

"Does it look like I give a damn?" I reply, crossing my legs and smiling at him. Leaning my chin on a palm to give him a good look at my eyes, I smile coyly. I'll win him over yet.

Grabbing a bottle from the cooler, he pops the top and puts a Budweiser on a coaster in front of me.

When a small bit of foam lands on my arm, I lick it and smile at him again. Still, his face doesn't show a hint of a smile. Stubborn man. He increases the volume on the television, which is showing some celebrity gossip show. The images of various famous couples and their preparations for Valentine's remind me of my own plans or lack thereof. I light a cigarette and ponder.

"Are you staying in here for dinner? We don't serve holiday dinners at the bar. I need to know if you want a table reserved."

"No, I'm having room service. I'm expecting someone," I answer, letting the cigarette burn without touching it.

"Can I ask why you do that with the cigarettes?"

On the TV screen is a picture of a Las Vegas casino and what appears to be Ray and a woman standing atop the steps of a main entrance, holding hands before cutting a ribbon. I mash the cigarette out with my thumb and feel a tear coming.

"No, you may not." I stand up. Throwing cash on the bar, I stride out of the room. I don't want him to see me cry. Walking to the elevator, I wipe the tear away. I don't have time to cry. I have preparations to make.

***

I shall wear the green dress since it's Ray's favorite color. First, I will lay in the bath for one hour. Routines are important to me. My father taught me about habit before I could shoot a gun. After my bath, I apply lotion all over my body until every inch is smooth. The scent of apricots fills the room as I dress and pull the stockings over my legs.

I have a bit of spare time before room service arrives. Should I write in my journal? Maybe write Ray a last minute letter? Do I have time for that? No, all of that is out of the routine. I need to brush my hair, to make it shine, to look my best. Can't disappoint Ray, can I?

In a few short months, I shall be in Vegas. The excitement builds up, but I want dinner to go off without a problem. I paid the man extra to make sure everything is perfect, but you never know these days. Service is terrible at best in most cities. Here is to hoping Dallas exceeds my expectations.

I hear a knock at the door, and my heart quickens. The night begins! Slipping on my pumps, I run to the door and look through the peephole. A bell-boy with a cart stands there. Opening the door, I lean against the frame, locking eyes with the boy and motioning with a finger for him to enter. He is small but not slight, and I like his light brown eyes, which keep darting about the room.

"Just you tonight?" the boy asks.

"Set the table as instructed. No questions." I cross my arms as the boy places the plates on the table.

With a pop, he opens a bottle of champagne and puts it on ice. He lights a candle on both ends of the table before moving a few feet away. I walk up to him. His shoulders tighten when I lean in and give him a kiss on his rosy cheek.

"Anything else?" His voice is scratchy and thin.

"That will be all." I walk him to the door and lock it behind him. Turning off the lights, I leave the room in candlelight.

I pour a glass of champagne and look over the table. There are two settings, both plates hidden by silver covers. The champagne adds to the drinks already consumed, and I feel heat in my face.

"It's time," I say to the room.

I lift the covers to reveal a dinner of seared lamb chops with asparagus and roast potatoes. The meal is perfect. I cut into the lamb and smile. It's rare, so the meat pulls away from the bone with little effort. My smile fades when the vision of the TV from earlier pops up in my head. I sample the meat but can't taste it. I feel tears again, and this time, I can't stop.

"The lamb is perfect, isn't it, Ray?" I whisper. My voice sounds odd. I'm struggling to swallow the food as tears begin to fall.

"I saw you with her, Ray." I manage to take a gulp of drink.

I force the meal down with more wine and then I sit as the candles burn.

"Ray, I hope you enjoyed dinner. Wait until you see my present."

There is no response. The empty room surrounds me, staring at me and putting lonely fingers around my throat.

"RAY!" I scream as loud as I can. I snuff out the candles with my fingers and lick the wounded skin before screaming again, "RAY!!!"

***

I can't stay in this room alone; I'm too upset. What did I see on TV? Is it politics? Is he lying to me? I'm not crazy or overreacting. *He stood there with another woman.*

124

Snatching my purse on my way out, I dash toward the elevator. It isn't until the elevator closes that I notice my reflection on the shiny door. I'm a mess with my mascara blotched from crying, which makes me look like a street walker. My attempt to fix my makeup results in smudging my eyeliner, making me look like a raccoon.

Keeping my head down, I nearly run through the lobby to reach the bar. I don't need to see the looks of the people shaking their head in judgment. I know what they're thinking, and I don't care. I'm the one suffering through the humiliation.

The bar isn't full, but there are enough people scattered about. Feeling comfortable that every eye isn't on me, I sit at the end on the last seat. The bartender sees me and smiles. I avoid his eyes. I feel shame for my behavior earlier and hope he doesn't make me sit in it for too long. Polishing a glass as he walks toward me, he still smiles, his eyes laughing in little wrinkles.

"What can I do you for?" he says, putting the glass into a rack.

"Coffee. Black," I sigh without looking up. Taking my phone out of my purse, I type a text.

"I'm afraid I don't have any coffee at this hour," he says.

I give in and look up at him. His eyes are a light hazel of brown and green. In spite of the anger and disappointment, I smile because it just dawns on me that he's very handsome. The thickness of his jaw encourages me to continue to watch him for a multitude of seconds. I like the way the stiff white shirt collar brushes against his jaw when he turns to the middle-aged woman sitting nearest to me.

The lady, who's wearing an awful combination of conservative and ugly, hogs his attention while I obsess over my looks. I have no idea if he thinks of me as anything more than a tip. Almost willing him to look at me again, I lean forward on my hand, staring without a care about what the awful lady is telling him. His eyes lock on mine even though he's still engaged in her story. The sneaky grin on his lips causes a little pit to form in my stomach, making me happy. Please, God, make her stop talking.

God must be listening because the lady leaves and Mr. Handsome Bartender looks my way. My mind starts to race in search of a comment, a piece of wit to impress him...anything. Nothing comes. Instead, I sit and stare, leaning on my hand and batting my eyes at him.

"Martini?" he asks.

His voice is deep and tickles my insides. With a nod, I watch him fix my drink. His hands move with precision, and his large arms flex with vigor as he shakes the tin before pouring the contents into the glass. Stabbing a few olives with a pick, he turns the drink with a flourish.

I take a gulp to calm my nerves, loving the feel of the alcohol numbing the insides of my mouth. It almost makes me forget for a moment that he stood me up on...no, I can't forget that, can I?

"Care to tell me about it?" He wipes and polishes the spot left by the lady.

"You wouldn't want to hear about it. It's about some stupid boy who stood me up tonight," I say.

"Quite right. I don't want to hear about any of that."

I stir the olives into the drink and watch him—waiting and wondering what he'll say to me next. Please...say something.

"Despite not being a makeup artist, you have the most beautiful eyes I've ever seen."

I laugh and can't stop. Did he really say that? Oh, but I'm smiling. He's a devil and knows it, the handsome shit!

"Does that line work for you?" I take another sip of my drink.

"Usually." Already making another drink, he whisks the empty away with a melodramatic flair.

"Do I look that easy?"

"No, I believe I said you're beautiful. And I want you to spend the night with me." His smile fades, and his eyes twinkle.

I feel him looking at my dress and wish the bar didn't hide me from the waist down. "What about right now?"

Looking behind him at the array of bottles and taps, he speaks to the room. "Seems I'm out of Absolut. I need to get another bottle."

He walks toward the kitchen, and I follow him at a distance. As we enter through a door to the left of the kitchen, I hear a lock click. I peek my head into the room and laugh—a storage closet. He's leaning against a row of bottles, waiting for me. When I step into the room, he replaces the lock and secures it before pushing me against the wall.

"Are you going to fuck me now?" I ask.

"Shh," he whispers, putting an arm around my waist and grinding against me. Placing his lips against my neck, he covers my skin with slow, tender kisses. His fingers trace over my arms in circles and pushes me back when I try to press into him.

"No teasing," I pant.

"Shh." He smiles, blowing against my ear and running his hands over my dress.

He continues to touch me and explore my body. As a hand finds my lower back, he pulls me into a kiss. His lips crush into mine, tasting me. We kiss for a while as his hands continue to rub and pinch and caress, making me moan into his mouth.

"Now, please," I plead with him.

With a smile, he sits on a keg and holds out a hand, which I accept. He pulls my hand, and I straddle him. I dig my hands into his thick brown hair, grinding on him with urgency. Lifting my dress, his hands find my ass and helps me push against his excitement. I close my eyes, letting the feeling flow over me—the savage need to press his hardness against that exact spot.

I pop the snap that secures his work pants, taking the warmth in my hands. I move my hips closer and guide myself on top of him.

"Slowly," he whispers into my ear.

I can't stop. "No, now," I grunt as I plunge down on him with such force it pushes the breath from my chest.

The keg rocks against the floor in staccato protest when I pull his hair to help me and guide me. The sound of my skin against his echoes through the room. He grips the cage for balance as I ravage him and use him like a toy. He's mumbling something, but I ignore him, feeling my orgasm building. I slow my pace to a near grind and pause each time I engulf him. My feet shake with effort and want of release.

A moment before I climax, I see an image of Ray in my mind. As I shudder against the bartender's shoulders, I feel a hint of anger building, which slaps a damper on a moment I didn't want him to spoil.

"Where are you?" His hands caressing my back, and he tries to look into my eyes.

I stand and adjust my dress, ignoring his question and his attempts to penetrate my mind.

"Come to my room after your shift ends," I say before walking out of the room.

BIRTH

The water is scalding hot. I lean against the tiles, letting it run over me and trying to gather the pictures of the day into something resembling a story. Could I tell it in a sentence to someone reading? I'm not sure. After I returned to the room and changed out of the dress, I wrote a few pages in my journal before the need to shower overtook me.

Getting out of the shower, I wrap a towel around my hair and let the water drip from my body. I find the lotion and go into the other room, wishing to watch TV through my beauty routine. The journal sits on the desk against the wall. I fight the urge to take a look at the last few pages and pick up my purse instead. I feel the knife through the fabric and pull back the zipper. Grabbing the black knife, I toss it onto the bed and dump the contents of my purse on the table next to the TV.

I place my brush, lotion, and makeup on the table. Since I'm not sure when the guy will arrive, I decide not to rush. Might as well look my best, no? I flip the TV on and am relieved that the gossip show makes no mention of my Valentine's Day horror.

Out of curiosity, I change to a financial channel, but there's an infomercial running. It promotes a revolutionary hair care product for women, so I watch, transfixed by both the amazing utility of the hair piece/comb and the reasonable price of $19.99.

Taking the towel from my head, I reach for my brush and hear a knock at the door. I walk to it and turn the lock.

"Count to five and come in, I'll be changing in the bathroom," I say before running from the room. I hear the door open and his greeting, but I can't hear his words through the door.

"Sorry to keep you waiting so long, a few customers didn't want to leave," he says again.

"It's quite okay. Make yourself a drink. There is a bottle of whiskey on the desk. I'll be right out."

I hear a glass clink against a bottle and begin brushing my hair. Standing against the door as I brush, I listen for noises from the other room but hear nothing more. A few minutes pass while I try my best to hurry my routine.

"Shit!" I curse, remembering I left the makeup on the table.

I can feel the heat rising in my cheeks. I hate when every detail isn't perfect. Pulling on a pair of boy-shorts and a white T-shirt that doesn't reach my waistline, I open the door and find him sitting at the desk. A sudden weakness attacks my knees as I watch him flipping the pages of my journal. I grip the door for strength. Standing still, I watch for a while, unable to process the information.

Managing to put a foot forward, I walk into the room. He stops reading and gazes up at me. I walk without hurry but a certain purpose. Taking the book from his hands and placing it back on the desk without a word, I gulp some whiskey. The clock sounds the hour, and the infomercial ends. I flinch as

131

I see a pretty commentator who reads the breaking news.

"Rumors that the trust of investment mogul, Ray Holden, taking a stake in beleaguered MGM have been heard for some time, but SEC filings in the last week have given more credence to the reports."

"I don't know where to begin..."

I snap back into the present. "Begin with why you were going through my journal. I figure a bartender might be better at staying out of my personal effects."

"Is that *your* Ray?" He gestures to the TV.

I walk away without a reply and head toward the table for my makeup. As I look back at him, I push the knife under a pillow.

"The one and same," I respond, grabbing my lipstick and eyeliner.

Walking by him to reach the bathroom, I wait for him to speak while I put on my makeup. I can see in the mirror that he's back to looking at my journal. A rush of anger shoot through my veins. I keep applying the red to my lips and try to ignore his violation.

"I can't help thinking this is true," he mutters.

Joining him once more, I pour another drink and sit on the bed. His eyes are probing me as if he's searching for answers.

"Do I look pretty?" I try to sound perky.

His jaw clenches as he grips the journal with his hands. Nevertheless, his eyes contain desire as they travel over my legs.

"I should leave." But he makes no motion to do so.

Crossing my legs and leaning back on my elbows, I wait for him to act. He stands and approaches the bed, his movements stiff, his eyes still pinned to my body. Reaching his hand toward me, he caresses my knee.

"The things I read can't be true," he says.

I'm not sure if he's trying to convince himself or expects me to verify, but I don't answer. His hand moves higher on my leg, his palm gripping my thigh, which is still moist from lotion. Finishing my drink, I place the empty glass on the floor. I move backward on the bed and put my head on the pillow.

"Come here. Forget about all that," I demand.

He sits on the bed next to me with his eyes running over my body. His hands begin to rub at will, traveling without permission or warning.

"I need to..." he mumbles.

I interrupt by gripping his tie and pulling him on top of me. His weight shifts onto my body, engulfing me in warmth.

"Just be with me tonight. No questions." I wrap my arms around him and squeeze him against my chest.

His face is close, and I can feel the alcohol on his breath. I can see red in his eyes and realize he's drunk. I shiver at this situation.

"Did that happen with your father?" he asks, ignoring my request.

"Don't mention him, please," I snap. I keep squeezing him, hoping to shut him up.

He becomes still and stares at me with curiosity in his eyes.

"It's okay to play me, but you can't answer me?"

Feeling him begin a slow grind against my leg, I try to push him away from me. "Maybe you should just go."

He's far too large for me to move and pushes into me, breathing against my neck. Making an attempt to roll to my side, I grunt with the effort. It only serves to deepen his grip on me. He pins my shoulders against the bed, and I cease to struggle.

"Get off me," I say.

"No," he grunts, taking my chin to face him. "You can't play with people like this. Life isn't a game."

"Fuck you," I yell. I hear the sound of his palm connecting with my face before the pain hits me. It spreads like fire over my skin.

"Like your father," he says with spit falling from his lip onto my cheek.

I slip my hand under the pillow and open the blade as he continues to mash his body against mine.

"Stop, please."

Ignoring me, he kisses me roughly on the neck before biting my ear. "Is it true? Did you enjoy it with your father?" He pulls his pants lower.

I begin to fight again, keeping my grip around the handle and hoping to push him off somehow. He slaps me again, so I dig my nails into his cheek. As he uses a hand to pull down my shorts, I try to squeeze my legs closed.

Feeling him against my leg, I begin to panic and swing at him. He forces my legs open and I scream, which makes him put his hand over my mouth.

"No, no, no!" I scream into his hand. As I feel him enter me, a tear runs down my face, and I struggle to breathe.

"Did you like it?" he asks again.

I can't take any more when he slams full inside me. I bite his skin. He yelps and pulls his hand away.

"Yes," I scream as I swing my free arm and bury the blade in his neck up to the hilt.

Blood sprays over my face, so I turn my head to avoid the worst of it. His hands claw at his neck, and choking sounds escape his throat. I pull the knife out and hear the blood squirting from the wound— jetting out in dark red streams through his fingers. I stab him again closer to the shoulder blade and twist, driving the blade up and into his esophagus.

He rolls off of me, grunts turning to feeble gasps of pain escaping his lips. The blood flow is immense and soaks into the sheets, causing me to jump from the bed. I pull the T-shirt over my head and run to the table to grab my cell phone. Pressing the stored number, I put the phone against my ear. A voice answers, and I watch the last of the man's life spilling out onto the bed. His hands are frozen at his throat.

"What is it, Ella?" the voice says, a man's voice I recognize, but can't place.

"I need help. I killed a man," I say in a rush.

There's a pause, and I hear whispering on the other end, but I can't make out the words.

"I'll be there in fifteen minutes," the voice says.

LOST IN NEW MEXICO

Looking west from Albuquerque, which seems to end so suddenly that it feels as if there's an invisible wall marking the city limits, I can't help staring into the wasteland of empty space. I want to lose myself in that vast space and in the nine hours of road between this city and Las Vegas. I want to hide from myself. Sitting in this café with a blank notebook open in front of me, I struggle to breathe, to think, or even to wonder what is happening to me.

What happened is clear in my mind. The pictures of that night, that moment, replay in sepia tones. Did it really happen? Any of it? Blood on my hands again?

My coffee is cold, but I can't seem to bring myself to signal the young boy with greasy, black hair behind the counter to order a new one. The room is empty except for an older gentleman sitting against the window, who's busy with his laptop. There are no distractions—nothing to save me from the thoughts crowding my brain.

How did I come to be here? I drove for hours, not knowing or caring about the direction. Somehow, when I got tired, I ended up in this city, one I never thought about before last evening. The hotel contains no restaurant or bar, so here I sit and wait to write and to dispel the constant nagging in my brain that my life is now forever altered.

The details of that night overtakes me. I feel his blood on my skin, dripping down my stomach like lava running over my body. I hear him asking that question again and again.

'Did you like it?'

I shake my head, but I hear his question again. *Did you like it?*

The hour that followed those moments of horror with him remains a blur, but I recall the face that appeared at the door to rescue me. How he arrived so fast is a mystery, but I was too occupied with escaping the scene to ask.

The door of the café opens, letting a man in a leather jacket and sunglasses enter. With a computer bag over his shoulder, he looks me over as he approaches the counter. I can't tell if he is still looking at me because I'm glancing down at my pink sweatpants and sweatshirt. I feel awful from the drive, overwhelming emotion, and lack of sleep. Placing the pen against the paper, I write the first line of the day.

A beautiful man walks into a café with sunglasses to keep the girl from seeing his eyes, but she feels his stare through the dark shades.

Taking the coffee offered to him by the young boy on duty, he slides into the seat opposite mine and pushes his chair close to the table. I'm sure he's looking at me while he unzips the bag and removes a notebook. It resembles mine, plain black with small rings binding the paper.

He's bold because he sits at the table with her even though there are many empty seats...

"Hello," he says.

I look up. He can't want me, not looking like this with my hair back and bound with pink barrettes. Without a reply, I tap my pen on the paper with my bare foot rubbing against the base of the table. They've slipped out of the flats I was wearing. The pen is against the paper again, but the words desert me. I return to staring out the window. I wonder how many bodies are buried out there—in the space between cities where the law and people don't exist.

"Hello," he says again, waving his hand in front of my eyes.

With a grunt, I acknowledge him with a nod. What does he want from me? Can't he see that I'm busy brooding or writing or whatever it is people do at cafés?

I sigh and slam my pen on the table. Pushing my chair out and standing, I try to push my foot into my shoe. Adjusting a loose barrette, I walk to the counter and order another coffee. His gaze still follows me. Why today? Why? I can't take it today, and I swear I'll make a scene before I deal with another damned man trying to...

"Can I help you?" the boy asks.

I mutter a curse and order, chewing my lip. Now, the older gentleman against the window is watching me, too. I feel like screaming. Can I just be me for one day? Men want and want and want, and I can't seem to get one to listen. I am a person, not a blow-up doll. Some days, I wish I were born ugly. Like today.

Bringing the coffee to the table, I stare at the man with sunglasses, hoping he'd look away. I take an angry sip and yelp as it burns my tongue and the roof of my mouth. I jump in my chair.

"You lost your sandal again," the man chuckles.

When he removes the sunglasses, I see eyes that are as blue as my own. There are small wrinkles leading to his temples, a sign that he's older than I first thought.

"And?" I grumble, still mad from burning my mouth.

Leaning back in the chair into a comfortable position, he takes a deliberate look under the table. "You have pretty feet."

I look up at the ceiling and feel the beginnings of a tear in my eye. I can't cry in front of him. Grabbing my pen, I write.

Another moth to the flame, ready to be burned alive. The girl smiles inside and wonders. Can it be so easy?

"Creepy," I sigh. I mimic him by crossing my arms, pursing my lips.

"I'm trying to be nice. I guess I can follow you from a more discreet distance. I just figured it'd be better if we didn't have to go through that whole game." His words spew out.

The temperature rises a few degrees. I feel his glare on me, touching me, probing me. I realize that I'm holding my breath, so I exhale and cross my legs. "Following me, eh? I'm guessing you aren't a fan."

His smile widens while his pale blue eyes dig into mine. He nods and sips coffee. The smile remains on his face.

The moth speaks secrets and laughs at the girl. She looks at him, as if for the first time, seeing the wind-chafed skin of his cheeks and thick stubble on his chin.

"Are you staying in the same hotel?"

He nods once again in the affirmative and remains silent.

"Then you know where I will be." I begin to gather my things, but he puts a hand on my wrist, holding me in place without being rough.

"What did you write?" he asks.

"Why do you care?"

He taps a finger on his own notebook, which seems to be all the explanation he's going to give. I turn the notebook over to him, not caring if he reads it.

He does, and a hint of a smile creeps on his thick lips. "I've never been called beautiful. I don't think. Thank you," he says, pushing the notebook back in my direction.

I look away from him, avoiding his gaze. I put the notebook into my bag and stand, this time, with no interference. Walking past him toward the door, I pause and turn to him.

"What happened to your partner?" I ask.

***

I knew he looked familiar though I can't believe I didn't remember. The only explanation is the trauma of the mass shooting. No matter. I know now and can't forget what I need to do. I wonder how much he knows about Dallas. Does he *know*? If he did, simply following me wouldn't have been his course of action. None of what he might or might not be aware of forms much importance. I must escape again.

Gathering and packing my possessions, I put clothes and writing materials into my backpack. I try to keep focus. I know he'll be watching me. He might even anticipate my escape, so I just can't walk out the hotel lobby to my car. My hand touches the knife when I hear a knock upon the door. I tiptoe across the carpet and look through the peephole. Marcus is standing in the hallway, waiting with his arms crossed.

"I'm getting dressed. Come back in an hour and I'll have room service. What can I order you?" I say, hoping this will provide me enough of a diversion.

"Steak. Rare," he says before walking away.

Leaning against the door, I exhale and gather my wits. I stride to the phone and call room service, ordering two steaks with sides and pie for dessert. Can there be a doubt he'll check to see that I placed the order?

There's a fire escape within reach, and I know I'll be able to reach the ground. Hurrying to pack the rest of my stuff, I see a map on the coffee table. I smile, thinking about pulling the same trick twice. I circle Las Vegas with a magic marker and place a star over Harrah's Casino. I doubt it will mean much other than to make him think I'm going to Vegas, which, of course, is true.

Nothing more needs to be done. I open the window and let the cold air lick my face as I reach for the fire escape with my toes. I can't quite reach it, so I'll have to jump. Tying the backpack tightly, I brace myself and leap. Hand latching onto the guard rail, I slide down to the base, leaving me hanging. My stomach lurches while I try to pull myself up, but I can't resist looking down. It's only about fifteen feet to the ground.

Giving up on lifting myself onto the fire escape, I let go. My feet smash on the concrete, and a jolting pain shoots down my legs. I clamp a hand over my mouth to muffle my cries while I check my knees and ankles to see if I broke anything. Managing to stand up, I walk as fast as possible toward my car, not bothering to look around. Either he sees me or he doesn't. There's nothing more I can do about it.

I really wish I had another car, but there's no time to secure one. I must leave at this very moment. I also don't have the luxury of plotting a path to Vegas that avoids major roads, so I take I-40 West with the plan of stopping in Gallup to hunker down. I know he'll stop in every town to look for me, so I'll have to use cash. Cash goes a long way in America, and it doesn't leave a trail. We don't speak English in America; we talk in *money*.

After a few miles, I stop checking the rearview mirror every few seconds. Again, I have to remind myself. Either he knows, or he doesn't. Driving within the speed limit, I flip on the radio and find a news channel. I wonder if my name might be mentioned. Am I wanted? Do they know? Or is he still trying to put the pieces together? My pulse quickens as the radio announcer mentions the upcoming breaking news.

Increasing the volume, I wait for doom. Sweat pours down my forehead into my eyes during the commercials. I wipe my face with a shirt, trying to keep my focus on the road. Finally, the announcer tells of a mass shooting at a church. I yell in frustration. I feel dirty that the sense of relief flows through my veins. No, I don't feel happy those people are shot instead of me. Why are there so many shootings in this country? I feel like a hypocrite, but I find the violence sickening.

I shut off the radio and drive silently toward Gallup. It seems I have made a clean escape. Not a soul shares the road on this cold winter night in February, and I feel more alone than I have in my life. No sign of Mr. Brown. I haven't seen Ray in years, and now I'm being chased across America by an FBI man that thinks I have nice feet.

It only takes two hours through dark desert to see a sign telling me I'm five miles from town. I search for hotels on my phone. There are a few national names, but it's probably safer to go with a smaller one. I'll more likely be able to pay with cash and find a place to stash my car.

I find one and book a room. At least I can relax for now, having a place to stay for the night. I'll take care of hiding my car in the morning. I hope staying in an out of the way lodge will throw Marcus off for a few hours. I can do nothing more than hope.

As my mind flitters over images of Ray and Mr. Brown, a sudden burst of thought pushes itself to the forefront. I arrive in Gallup, New Mexico. The memory of the day I met Ray surfaces in my mind.

GALLUP, NM

The sign is in disrepair, and in the darkness, I can only make out the Motel part. From the outside, it looks rundown. I contemplate driving off in search of a better hotel, but I remind myself that this place is a perfect hideout. Nearby, two men in dirty jeans and jackets are in the middle of a drug deal. This has to be the place. It looks more like a laundromat than a motel with the bright lights, plain tile floors, and open space.

A middle-aged man behind the desk watches me from behind his thick glasses. I wait for him to stand.

"You look a little young for a room. Must be 21," he says without much care.

He flips through a newspaper without paying me much attention, almost as if he's trying to anger me. Well, I couldn't care less about his attitude or his rule because I know he'll like what I'm about to offer. Taking my purse out of my bag, I slap a few hundred dollar bills on the counter.

"I seem to have lost my identification."

He studies my face. "Are you running from the cops?"

I pause to hide my laughter. No, he isn't a cop. Not exactly, anyway. "Listen, Mister, I don't want to get into the whole sordid thing. Long story short, there may be a man looking for me. So, I'd much rather he not find me if that's okay with you."

"What's he want with ya?" He quickly scoops up the money and fishes for a set of keys.

"He thinks I have cute feet," I say.

He comes round the counter and heads for the door. I'm not sure if he wants me to follow, so I stay where I am. Looking back at me, he indicates with a nod to come with him. I cautiously follow him while keeping my eyes on the people leaning against buildings doing nothing on the right side of the law. Leading me to a door, he looks me over.

"Well, is it true?"

"What's that?" I tilt my head in confusion.

"Do you have cute feet? I'd like to see."

I resist the urge to vomit and take the key from him. "Do you happen to have a garage I can rent to store my car while I'm in town? I'd rather park it somewhere safe."

Sniffing my hair, he whispers, "You don't smell like a cop, so I guess if you have a couple more of those hundreds I could find a place to stow your car."

I put three more bills into his dirty, rough hand along with my car keys, not caring if he steals it. There's nothing of value in the car, anyway. He scurries away, smiling and snickering to himself. Yeah, five hundred dollars will make anyone happy. I don't know if he'll be trouble, but I'm betting he won't talk to the cops or anyone else about me. If anything, he'll show up later for himself.

My room is ordinary with a large bed in the center with matching side lamps and a desk against the wall that I place my backpack on. A TV is against the far wall, and a mini-fridge and a coffee maker fill out the last of the furniture in the room. I can't help but approve of the frugality and only wish for something to drink.

Remembering the men dealing drugs, I take a single hundred from my purse and march outside. It doesn't take long for a man of middle age to approach me.

"What can I do to you?" he asks.

Gag. I flash the bill before stuffing it back into my parka. "What can I get to smoke for that?"

"All that just to smoke you up, shorty? You too young to be a cop. What you out here by yourself for? Ain't you got a man?"

"I don't need one. I need some weed. Can you help or not?" I say, in no mood for yet another man to give me his lines.

As if sensing what I'm trying to tell him, he walks into the shadows. I follow in silence, palming the money and ready to give it to him. Without a word, he slips me a baggie, and I put the money into his waiting hand. Not bothering to look at it, I return to the room and bolt the door shut.

I waste no time and pack the pipe for much needed release. This grimy town is unsettling, to say the least. I wonder how much of America resembles this place when a train rattles the walls with horns blaring and tearing the night. Shots ring out as I take a hit, but I don't care. It doesn't matter to me. Just another dead hooker or junkie...or a cop.

It's an endless parade of deaths across this land of ours. Some say there are about 300 million guns in private possession in America. I find that hard to believe. Is violence in our blood? Are we born murderers? Or is something in the American experience particular in bringing out the savage in us all? There can be no doubt we have more murders than the rest of the civilized world by a great margin.

Sirens pierce the night as I take another rip of the bowl. I put my earphones into the phone, letting Pink Floyd take me away from the madness surrounding me. Ah, that's better. I can relax and let the stress wash away.

Is anybody out there? I know it's stupid to ask while I'm high, but I wish someone might answer. Where are you, Ray? Why am I stranded and hiding in this drugged-out town in the middle of nowhere? Why am I alone? Are you with her tonight?

The wind blows and the medical personnel haul the dead bodies off to wherever they need to be taken. Where are you right at this moment? Do you realize I'm only seven hours from Las Vegas? Don't you know that soon whatever situation you are in will have to change?

Over the music, I hear a noise at the door and turn down the volume. Again. I hear it and there can be no mistake. Someone's knocking on my door.

"Hello, I know you're in there," I hear a voice say.

Looking through the peephole, I see the hotel man standing in wait for me. He's hiding a bottle of alcohol of some kind in his jacket. Part of me knows I shouldn't open the door. What good can come of it? Another part of me whispers lies, that perhaps he talked to Marcus and letting him inside may give me clues to the whereabouts of my stalker. Urges flood into my veins, and the images of blood and guts covering the room appears. My hand turns the knob and opens the door.

"What can I do for you, sir?" *Sir means dead man. If you could read my thoughts...*

He turns the bottle toward me, smiling at me with crooked yellow teeth. I shake my head at his choice of wine, white zinfandel.

"I thought you might need someone to stay with you tonight. You know, just in case any unsavory characters knock on your door."

A cold breeze ruffles my flower print pajamas and I shiver, but I doubt that it's only from the temperature. He's a moth to the flame, and I won't let him in. I will resist this temptation. *You should run from me, sir. You will not get what you desire in this room.* Why can't I tell him to buzz off and leave me alone? Can I do this? Passing this test can only help me learn to control what I feel inside. This man means nothing to me, and I don't have to...

"A little wine might help me sleep. Come in," I say, moving aside to let him enter, closing and bolting the door behind him.

He stands near the bed while he scans the room, gaze stopping at my writing materials on the desk.

"Doing schoolwork?" he asks.

"Writing a novel." I shoot a sharp glance at him.

"Oh. What's it about?" he asks, opening the micro-fridge and removing plastic cups. He opens the bottle and pours me a cup of wine.

Can I tell him what my book is about in one sentence? I've always heard that if you can't describe your book this way, perhaps you need to go back to the drawing board. So, what am I writing about? Good question. Taking the cup from him, I swallow half of it in a gulp to avoid the metallic taste of the cheap, sweet wine. Heat flows to my face, and I blink to fight a wave of dizziness. The man talks, but I ignore him and practice various thesis sentences to describe my novel in my mind.

I prop myself on the bed and cross my legs at the ankles, taking another deep hit from the pipe. The man continues on and on and on about god knows what while I retreat deep inside, thinking about Ray and the day I met him. Tiny pictures of him working in that convenience store near my house cascade in my mind. I went to the store in search of candy that day without any money, which never stopped me because petty theft was as familiar as brushing my hair. I remember what I wrote about that day.

I noticed Ray the moment I entered the store. You're new, I thought to myself, and he was handsome with dark eyes and olive skin. He stared at me as I walked around in my cut-off shorts and no shoes, almost surprised at my bold sass as I tried to steal a candy bar right in front of his eyes.

What are you staring at? I asked him, not noticing a police officer who was standing a few feet away and leaning against a counter sipping on coffee. He hollered about not wearing shoes. I dropped the chocolate bar and ran from the store that instant. But my eyes met Ray's and I held his gaze for a moment that seemed to last...forever. Words will always fail me when I try to describe that day and that particular moment.

In retrospect, I'd say it was love at first sight, but at that time, I had no concept of the existence of love.

No matter. Something physical seemed to pass from him to me and me to him. Even though he spoke no words, I felt as if he reached into my mind to say: Hello there, beautiful.

Words stop as I feel the man lifting my pajamas a few inches. His fingers travel over my ankle and lower leg. I watch him with curiosity. A look at the clock tells me I spent almost thirty minutes thinking about Ray, and this is as far as he got? I neither encourage nor discourage, but instead, I sip at the wine to wet my mouth. It feels like I'm chewing a handful of cotton balls. If I lie here completely still, will anything happen at all? At this pace, this man seems unlikely to finish what little he got started.

He looks up at me, and it takes me a moment due to being so damn high to realize that he's tugging on my pajamas and managing to pull them over my hips. I almost feel proud of the sad, old man as he ever so slowly removes them, leaving me with only panties and my pajama top. Go on, little rabbit, right into the snare. Suddenly, my phone vibrates on the desk. It's three in the morning. Who could be calling at such an hour?

Perhaps, my location isn't a secret after all. This call can't be coincidence. The man continues while I check my phone. I expect a knock on the door or the window to explode followed by SWAT team. My imagination runs wild, wondering if they'll arrest me or simply riddle me with bullets. Though, like on television, won't they capture me alive to study me or pick at my brain?

The man climbs on top of me, naked from the waist down, pressing it against my leg. While he grips my shoulders and rubs on me, I hear my phone vibrate again. I wonder if I should just tell this man to leave. It might not be the best time for any of this. My hand grips the knife, and in that moment, my mind clears of all the noise. I can hear my thoughts again as I wait for him to cross that line, the one that will make me pounce into action. *Make me do it, sir. Can you feel even a hint of danger?*

Managing to get it inside me, he hugs his body against mine. I can't even tell if he's moving or not, that's how little he's doing. I feel an urge to say something, but he groans and pulls out, clutching me tightly, which causes me to tilt my head sideways in confusion. Warm wetness pools in my navel, and I growl in frustration. Less than two minutes? Are you fucking kidding me? You, sir, have brought ruin to this moment. I throw the knife on the nightstand in disgust and push him off me. I grab his pants, drag him to the door, and force him from the room. Latching the door once more, I stride to the phone and find a message from Mr. Brown. Tapping the screen, I read the text.

What are you doing with him?

So, I am being followed. I wonder if there's a transmitter in my car or my phone. I'll have to address that in the morning, but for now, I type a short reply.

Fuck off.

CHANGES

The financial channel plays in the background as I make notes in my journal. It will have to suffice for writing today because I plan on hitting the road the moment the hotel manager returns. I wasted a lot of the cash Ray gifted me to accomplish a few tasks I deemed necessary. The obvious fact is that I'm unable to escape Mr. Brown. It's almost noon, so I expect the manager back within the hour, certainly no later than two or three.

I suppose I can use this time to work on my book. Looking over what I wrote yesterday about the day I met Ray, I see that I left out Father's reaction to it all. Once I left the convenience store after meeting Ray, I ran home with the intentions of getting changed into more suitable clothing to satisfy the cop and going straight back to the store. However, Father was home and drunk, waiting for me.

"Where have you been?" he yelled, following me into my room and watching as I changed into a pink shorts and black Converse sneakers. *"Why are you changing? You aren't going out again. You're going to make me dinner."*

"I forgot my money and left stuff on the counter at the store. I'm going back there to get my candy," I

said, pushing by him to reach my closet and sifting through my clothes to find a matching top.

Grabbing my arm, he turned me to face him, breathing hot alcohol on my neck. "You aren't going anywhere," he growled.

I let my body go limp and waited for the anger to pass, looking into his eyes and smiling. "Yes, Daddy, I am. I'll come back and make your dinner. Then we'll watch TV, okay?"

"Why are you getting dolled up?"

I reached up and kissed his cheek, rubbing my hand along his shoulder. "Don't be jealous, Daddy. I'll be back before you know it."

I ran from the house before he could detain me any longer, running as fast as possible back to the store. The July heat slowed me as I climbed the hill. After waiting outside to catch my breath, I entered to see him by the soda machine, shaking his head.

"I can't believe this is happening," he muttered, still shaking his head.

"You can't believe what is happening?" I asked, feeling as if he's talking about me.

He spun around to face me with his mouth dropping open as he recognized me. I saw attraction in his eyes.

"I didn't hear the bell."

"I don't think it went off." I winked. "Do you like my shoes?"

I modeled for him, leaning on one leg then the other before spinning around slowly to let him look at my outfit. He stared in silence, which made me laugh. Then I grabbed the candy bar from before and held it up. When he nodded, I squealed with delight. Neither of us broke eye contact for so much as a moment, *which couldn't be played off or denied. I knew that he wanted me, and I loved it.*

Regardless, I needed to get home before Father came looking for me. I remember thinking that he can't know about this. Just before I took off, I realized that I didn't give him my name, so I ducked my head back inside the store. Our eyes met again and I let him take all the time he needs looking me over. That brought a wide smile on my face.

"I'm Ray, in case you want to know."

I giggled and winked once more. "I'm Ella."

A knock at the door stops me, and I shut off the tablet. This seems like the only writing I'll be able to do today. Through the peephole, I see the manager waiting for me with shopping bags. Opening the door, I pull him inside, making sure to bolt the lock.

"Well, were you followed?" I rummage through the bags, checking for the items I requested him to purchase.

"I didn't see anyone, but that doesn't mean I didn't have prying eyes watching me."

He eyes me as I take a pre-pay mobile phone from the bag and begin ripping it out of the plastic packaging. Turning on my phone, I type the numbers stored into the pre-pay, being sure to save them before I put it aside. The man puts a hand on my leg below the hem of my robe as I sit on the bed to inspect the new tablet he bought.

Ignoring his advances, I hit the power button on the tablet, being unfamiliar with both the brand and operating system. I send all my story files to my email and download them on the new tablet.

He puts a hand under my robe and I grab his wrist, stopping him. "You promised," he whines, adjusting his glasses with the other hand.

"After we finish our business. Now, tell me about the car situation." I sigh, releasing his arm.

"I found a college student looking to sell his Chevy Nova. It runs. From what I can see, it's in decent shape. It will certainly get you to Vegas."

"Perfect. Did you move my stuff into the trunk as I asked?"

"Yes, but don't you want to know how much I paid?" His hand moves higher and I lean back against the pillow.

"No. Keep the extra money. That was the deal."

He discovers my naked body under the robe and giggles. Rolling my eyes, I turn my head. At least this will be short...

***

The Nova starts with a rumble, and I can feel the engine as well as hear it. A smile comes to my face. I put the car in gear and give it a little gas, causing the engine to jump on command and launch the car onto the interstate. I wonder why the college student sold this car because it runs beautifully. I can only assume that he's a meth head or has a gambling problem.

Looking in the rearview for any sign of Mr. Brown's BMW, I'm relieved to see nothing but desert on all sides of me. I turn on the radar detector on the dashboard, which allows me to increase my speed to 80. At my present pace, I'll be in Vegas soon. I search for dance music to match my mood, but I can't find anything decent and decide to put in a Rihanna CD. Her music always reminds me of Ray.

With nothing other than music and thoughts of seeing Vegas filling my mind, my thoughts drift back to that early July when I met Ray. My plan of keeping a secret from my father didn't work for long, and a creepy irony came to pass when my father kept threatening to report Ray to the police every time I saw him. Indeed, my father discovered my crush the very next day.

I woke early that next day, July 3rd, 2004 and felt a rush of happiness when I realized my father already left for work. That meant I would have the day to myself and see Ray again at the store. I knew exactly what I wanted to wear and as I showered, imagined his reaction. After I brushed my hair and put lotion on my legs, I put on a short pink skirt, the heels Father bought for me, and a baby blue tank top. Looking at myself in the mirror, I knew Ray's eyes would pop out of his head when he saw me.

I arrived at the store just before one o'clock and asked the lady behind the register if Ray was working. She stared at my clothing and my eye makeup but didn't make a comment other than to tell me Ray was stocking the cooler. I told her I owed him money for a candy bar he bought me yesterday and walked to the back of the store. I opened the cooler and entered before my confidence could leave me.

Ray turned and dropped the gallon of milk he held when he saw me. His eyes widened at the sight of my bare legs and arms on display. I held out a dollar bill, smiling and leaning on one foot. I felt such joy at letting him touch my skin with his eyes and felt electricity pass into my hand when I put the money in his palm.

"You scared me," he said, voice shaking, his eyes roaming over my body.

"Don't be scared," I said as I lowered myself down to his level, balancing myself by sitting on my heels. I knew he could see under my dress and my pink cotton panties.

"You're going to get me in trouble."

"Why, do you have a girlfriend?" I gently placed a hand on his shoulder to keep balance.

"Sort of..." he mumbled, unable to pull his eyes from my legs.

"Well, I don't see her in here, so there isn't anything to worry about, Mister." I winked, trying to make him think I had it all under control, which, of course, I didn't. My heart raced at the thought of being discovered by his boss. Would he be arrested? Not wanting to take a chance, I stood up and backed away a few steps.

"I'll be on register at three, okay?" he pleaded.

I nodded and walked toward the door. "See you then, Ray."

I feel the pre-pay phone vibrating in my pocket and pull it out to see the name. It must be the hotel manager since he's the only one with the number. I contemplate not answering, but he might have information about Mr. Brown or even Marcus, so I hit the button to put him on speaker.

"Yes?"

"The man following you came in to ask questions a few minutes ago."

"So, he's still in New Mexico? Good. That puts me at least five hours ahead of him," I say, smiling. At least, a part of my plan seems to be working. "Thank you for all the help."

"No, thank you for this afternoon. I can't believe I got to—"

I don't need to hear a play by play of what happened. Why do men always feel the need to do that, to watch endless highlights of a game they just got done watching? No need to tell me the details. I was there, sir.

"You're breaking up, I have to go," I say, ending the call.

So, Mr. Brown is off my trail. The skyline of Vegas is in the distance, still some fifty miles away. I will enter Las Vegas without being seen and find out for myself what's going on with Ray and *the other woman*. First thing is to find out her name and then the where.

Increasing the volume, I sing along with the music and wonder when I can call myself Ray's girl. I don't know if I'll be the only girl in his life, but I plan on being the only one that matters. The song blares from the speakers as I cross the city limits. Welcome to Las Vegas, the sign says.

Welcome, indeed. Hello, Vegas. Wait until you get a load of me.

LAS VEGAS

I can't believe I'm in Vegas after driving for almost two months and thousands of miles. A bitter wind makes the temperature feel a lot colder than the 55 degrees promised by the weatherman on the radio. In reality, I don't know if my plan worked or if my location is secret, but I'll just have to keep going. I park the Nova in a garage at M casino at the very bottom of the city, planning on leaving keys in the ignition and hoping it will be stolen.

Putting the phone and tablet given to me by Mr. Brown on the seat, I walk away from the car and make my way to the front entrance of the casino. Before finding a taxi, I grab a map of Vegas from the visitor's display near the check-in desk. I get into the first one from a row of taxis. An older man sits behind the wheel and looks at me in the rearview mirror, waiting for me to give him a destination. Looking at the map, I pick a casino at random.

"Hard Rock Hotel," I say. I don't know why. Maybe because I love music.

Without answering, he pulls out into traffic and drives north on Las Vegas Boulevard. It doesn't feel like the strip down here because most of this bottom section is surrounded by desert waste the city hasn't gotten around to populating. I can see the lights and mass of buildings getting closer, and the first major casino coming into view is Mandalay Bay. Of all the attractions, I want to see the Bellagio first, which sits like a castle behind a moat of water.

I can't contain my excitement as the taxi passes the various casinos. The giant air balloon apparatus set up at Paris Casino catches my eye more than the Eiffel Tower replica. I want to dive into all I see and have a grand drunk week of tourist extravagance. Caesar's Palace seems massive from the outside with its Roman style columns of the Augustus Tower, and it makes me want to explore everything.

As I snap a picture of the Bellagio water show with my phone, it begins to buzz with a new text message. Interesting. I look at the screen and see the name of the hotel manager.

Smart getting a pre-pay. However, since I know your destination, it will not take me long to find you.
See you in Vegas,
Mr. Brown

I wonder what happened to the hotel man. The taxi turns into Hard Rock, which hangs a massive guitar that can be seen for a mile. I shake the thought from my mind. I can't worry about things out of my control, but I can't help thinking what he might have suffered to help me escape my stalkers. With one last shake of my head, I approach the front desk. The casino seems empty, and the man behind the desk quickly finds me a room.

"How many nights will you be staying with us?" he asks a casual question.

I don't actually have an answer at a moment like this. Indefinitely? Ray told me not to come to Vegas before July, which is some four months from now.

"Can I rent the room for a month?"

"At most, I can do ten days. Longer stays, you can negotiate with the manager during business hours. Will that be agreeable to you?"

"Yes." I hand him my bank card.

He swipes it on the machine and hands me a receipt, my room key, and a visitor's guide. I take it and make my way to the room. It contains an amazing view of the strip and a king-sized bed.

Tossing my stuff onto a chair, I collapse on the bed, feeling a wave of exhaustion from the drive and tension of the day. I could use some sleep, but I know that hunger will keep me up. Grabbing the phone from the nightstand, I press the button for room service.

"What can I get for you?" a pleasant voice asks me almost immediately.

I can get used to this treatment real fast. "Chicken fingers and fries with a lot of ranch."

"Any beverages?"

"Coke and Gatorade."

"That will be twenty minutes."

They work fast around here. I change out of my clothes and place my writing materials on the desk; my eyes fall on the mini-bar against the wall. Jackpot! But I have to wait until after the food arrives to attack the hoard, so I open my tablet, setting it up for later. A certain memory keeps repeating in my mind, and I must write it down soon before it drives me crazy.

I hear a knock and rush to the door, opening it without even bothering to look in the peephole. A young guy about my age stands there. I find him to be quite good looking and invite him inside, but he seems to want to finish the transaction in the hallway. In the movies, they always come in the room! Hello!

Following me, he carries the tray to the table near the bed and arranges the items one by one. Once he finishes, he stands aside, obviously looking to return to work. I guess my looks are ordinary for this city.

Sighing, I hand him the money and tell him he can leave. Oh, well. I have writing to attend to, anyway. I put my notebook next to my food and make occasional notes as I eat the chicken tenders, which are dry and salty. Grabbing a few mini-bottles of whiskey from the bar, I take a seat at the desk and prepare to write. My adventures and the wild, crazy journey that brought me to Sin City from NYC seem forever ago, when in reality it took less than two months to get here.

I am finally here in Vegas. Does Ray know? What does he think of my journey? Is my arrival a positive for him or yet another problem in his life? I can't answer any of those questions, but I can't get Ray out of my mind. In many ways, Independence Day all those years ago feels more vivid in my mind than the first days of my journey to Vegas. I shall remember it always as it will remain an important part of my life.

It was July 4th, 2004. The day started poorly with my father screaming at me to make breakfast to soothe his hangover. He drank more than usual the previous night due to having the 4th off. He seemed as if he was intent on making me suffer every minute. He consumed a copious amount of whiskey with his eggs. When I thought I couldn't take it for another minute, he finally passed out on the couch.

I got dressed and ran from the house as fast as possible before he could wake up. I wanted to see Ray. I didn't know if he'd be working, but I had nothing else to do and nowhere to go. The heat made sweat pour down my face. When I reached the store, I mopped my forehead with my T-shirt, revealing my stomach. No, I never cared much for being modest.

Pushing my way inside, I scanned for Ray but only saw a lady I didn't recognize behind the counter. She watched me curiously. I assumed it was because of the lack of customers.

"Is Ray working?"

"No, not today."

I felt like someone punched me in the stomach. So much for my hopes, I muttered under my breath. Was I doomed to spend the day with Father? The lady asked if I needed anything, but I simply shook my head and left. Sitting on the bench for a while, I let the sun cook my skin. I dreaded the thought of going home. I didn't even have enough money for an ice cream cone from the shop a block away. As I thought about what I could do other than go home, I saw Ray's blue Firebird pull into the parking lot.

My heart leapt with joy and relief. I ran to meet him, nearly tripping on the grooved cement near the gas pumps. I skidded into the door and put my elbows on the window.

"Whatcha doing?"

163

"Getting ice," he said, opening the door.

It forced me back a few feet. He seemed distant. I waited by his car while he went inside and came back out with two bags of ice in each hand. Dropping them on the pavement, he opened the trunk, pulled out a cooler, and began packing ice around the food and drink. He didn't look at me, as if he were purposely ignoring me.

"What's wrong?" My brows lifted.

"Nothing's wrong. You can't be talking to me like this. I'm not working, so we have no reason to speak."

I suddenly understood he was afraid to get in trouble. Leaning against his car, I looked around and didn't see a soul. Not a car or anyone walking. "Nobody is watching us, Ray. You have nothing to worry about."

He looked around and shrugged.

"Where are you going?"

"To see my father."

"Can I come with you?" I asked cheerfully.

His eyes finally met mine. I felt the no in his eyes, but on that day, I didn't plan on taking no for an answer. Without permission, I walked around to the other side of the car and got into the passenger's seat. If he wanted me out, he'd have to make a big effort. He put the driver's seat up, eyeing me before stowing the cooler in the back seat.

"You're going to get me in a lot of trouble," he said.

Still, despite his objection, he got in the car, shut the door, and started the engine. I kept quiet as he pulled the car onto a highway heading south. I curled my legs under me, watching him and hoping he liked my new tan, knee-length shorts, and pink t-shirt. He *turned on the radio to a rock station I like, which made me smile and content to watch him drive.*

"I promise I won't be any trouble, unless you want—" I started after some time as he exited the turnpike and navigated the twisting farm town roads of central Connecticut.

Without looking at me, he interrupted. "Enough of that talk. You're several years too young to be going on like that in front of a man my age. Wait until you're twenty-one."

"I'll be an adult at eighteen."

"Yes, but I don't find myself in the company of anyone that isn't of drinking age very often. So, as I said, come back to me at twenty-one with that sort of talk."

I considered his comment for a moment, letting the music fill the void. "Is that a promise?"

"Sure," he said.

"I'll hold you to that, sir."

He smiled as he eased the car to a stop outside the gates of a very large white mansion, which sprawled up and around a hill. A multitude of buildings surrounded the main structure. Shutting off the engine, he opened the door and approached the guard house attached to the gate. He pressed a button, and a voice sounded through the metal box.

"Who lives here?" I whispered.

"Father," he said.

A knock at the door makes me put the notebook on the table. I can't help grunting in frustration, for I detest interruptions when I'm writing. Through the peephole, I see a stranger. I can only assume the man is lost or knocking on the wrong door, so I wait until he leaves before stepping into the hallway. Did Mr. Brown send him? Did Marcus? One thing seems clear to me. I'd better not waste my time alone in Vegas in my hotel room. What if I'm caught before I have a chance to see any of the sights and sounds of this exciting city? I simply can't let that happen.

Returning to the bedroom area, I put on a thick dress that will keep me warm on this Vegas winter night. Looking in the mirror and adjusting my makeup, I feel a sudden surge of excitement building up. I'm going out in Las Vegas tonight!

***

What would a person do in Las Vegas if there was only one night? I'm left with sixty-eight dollars, which won't last very long, for sure. Is it possible to have fun without money and without being twenty-one? I shall soon find out. Months of anticipation culminate in one night on the city. As I exit the hotel, the same question pops up in my head. Where is Ray tonight?

Excitement fills my veins as the taxi follows the line toward Las Vegas Boulevard. Lights rise and illuminate the darkening sky. Bellagio sits like a castle behind a large moat lake. I take my time to exit the taxi after it stops near the front entrance. I don't want to miss a thing. The lights, sounds, and a crowd entering the large turnstile doors usher me inside. I find myself gawking at the winter display alongside the rest of the tourists, pulling my mobile to snap a few pictures.

The endless ringing of bells sounds off from every direction to announce the latest slot victory. Stopping to watch a man tap a touch screen video poker machine for five bucks a hand, I wonder if I'll get carded if I sit at a machine. Though I can't afford to play for long, I wouldn't mind joining in on the fun. Moving along the aisle towards the poker room, I spot an open slot machine advertising 25-cent poker and sit.

I put a ten into the machine, light a cigarette, and choose the game. Jacks or better poker. The first few hands lose, and I shake my head. Why do people love playing these machines? It seems a bit monotonous. As I tap the screen again, a waitress appears at my side, yelling about cocktails. Without thinking, I ask for a Jack Daniels with Coke. She returns with the drink in short order and accepts the tip in silence. Her service may be efficient, but the drink isn't strong. But it's only a dollar. Even with my depleting funds, I should be able to have some fun when the drinks are this cheap. I shall enjoy Vegas for sure!

A commotion from the poker room draws my attention, so I stand to get a better view. Several players at one table are standing with two of them are 'all-in' the dealer says. For how much? I begin counting the chips, but before I can get a handle on how much, the dealer declares a winner and sweeps the pile toward a cheering Asian man. The man catches my gaze and smiles as he begins stacking the chips into neat rows.

Returning my attention to the machine, I begin clicking again. The monotony continues and I drink another cocktail. Finally, excitement comes when the game deals me three of a kind. Before I click the deal button, I look on the payout screen to see that four of a kind pays 50-1! A man stops behind me, watching me play over my shoulder.

"Say one time."

"One time," I repeat and click the button. Before I see the result I hear the bells sound and know I have won. Four eights, winner! The machine tells me I have 88 credits, and my heart starts to pound. "How much did I win?"

The man reaches over my shoulder and taps the spot telling me the credit total and it switches into a monetary display. Twenty two dollars. I am rich! The man laughs at my excitement and pats me on the shoulder.

"You have to play max bet for the progressive," he says, pointing at the number display above the machine, which keeps increasing by the moment like the debt counter in Times Square.

"I can't afford that, sir."

With a laugh, the man reaches into his pocket and removes a thick wad of bills. He peels off a single hundred and stuffs it into my machine. "Welcome to Vegas."

"Thank you, sir," I say as he takes a seat on my left.

He inserts money into the machine and begins clicking at a fast rate, seeming to need only a moment to see the cards before making a decision. "Do you have plans for the evening?"

The question catches me by surprise and so do his pale blue eyes watching me. What exactly are you asking me? I don't know if I'm paranoid due to being followed across the country, but I can't help thinking he could be a cop.

"I have no plan. I'm just looking for adventure and will let it happen as it will," I speak matter-of-factly.

"I see," he says, examining me. "Are you sure you aren't looking for someone or waiting for something?"

What do his questions imply? I pause to decipher his words. Does he think I'm a prostitute? That must be it. That would also mean...

"Nothing like that, sir. I'm just a girl alone in Vegas, trying to have a good time." This time, I try to sound perky and upbeat.

"Be careful about having too good a time. Vegas can be a dangerous place for a beautiful girl."

With his warning tossed aside, I spin the chair toward him and cross my legs in torn blue jeans. "Thank you for the compliment, sir."

"Your beauty is a fact, not an opinion. No more thank me for mentioning it than credit a scientist for acknowledging the existence of gravity."

Um...is he really this dull? "Are you staying at the Bellagio?"

"No, I'm a local."

"Are you a cop?"

"Yes."

Breathe, just breathe. The sounds of the room spin in my head as I try to stop hyperventilating. What do I say to him next? Sweat drips down my side as I tap at the screen over and again, not caring about the results. After a few minutes, I stop. My balance in the machine tops three hundred dollars, and the man smiles as I tap the cash-out button. He follows as I walk to the redemption machine and turn my ticket into money. Without a word, I extend a one hundred dollar bill towards him, as if that will be explanation enough.

"That's yours. Buy yourself a drink or ten."

Can he arrest me? Will he? I shake my head. Did I do anything illegal? Is taking money from a stranger a crime? I feel his presence in the distance, casually taking pictures of the lobby like a tourist. Outside, the temperature fell a few degrees, so I pull my jacket tight around my neck. I mix into the crowd along the sidewalk leading to the street with the lights and music signaling the beginning of another water show.

I stop and lean against a lamp post to watch the display of water, music, and light interwoven in a seamless way, the streams of light and blasts of water timed to match various points of emphasis in the song. The cop leans against the same lamp post and places his elbows on the concrete railing, pretending to concentrate on the show. I hum along with an Italian song made popular by an American television show about gangs out of New Jersey.

"Con te partiro..." he sings in a pleasant bass tone to accompany my humming.

The water show ends and I start moving. Again, I follow tourists onto the street, knowing the cop is close behind me. As I wait for the crosswalk light, the cop moves quite near me, sending a shiver down my body.

Without turning toward him, I blurt out for all around us to hear, "I'm trying to have a night out in Vegas, so can you please stop following me?"

My words don't seem to matter to him because he continues to follow me toward Planet Hollywood. The wind increases in intensity, and I wish I wore the thicker parka instead of the windbreaker. Stopping to look up at the casino, the man bumps into me. I sigh. Why does this shit always happen to me? Pushing him out of my way, I signal for a taxi. I might as well hold the door open for him. He's not giving up any time soon. He hops in without a word and smiles. I give the address to the cabby and we're off to Hard Rock.

The short ride ends without either of us having spoken and I exit the car. I lead the way inside and push my way through the drunken crowd toward the elevator with the cop at my side. He hums a tune I do not recognize while the elevator whisks us to my floor.

"I don't suppose you'll wait outside?" I insert the key into the lock.

He snorts and follows me into the room, letting out a low whistle as he surveys the space surrounding us. "I like what you've done with the place."

Grabbing a few mini-bottles of booze from the micro-fridge, I join him in the sitting area. I stop in my tracks as I see Mr. Brown sitting on a recliner in the shadows along the wall. A handgun with a silencer sits on his lap as one hand pulls at his beard. Fear and shock hit me. The cop doesn't see him yet. Am I about to be killed? My eyes lock with Mr. Brown's as he rises to his feet, one hand gripping the gun.

"I think it's time for you to leave, Officer."

I watch as Mr. Brown closes the distance between them. One of his arms slides around his neck and hold him in a choke hold. His arms flail as

Mr. Brown squeezes and squeaking noises escape his lips.

"No, Mr. Brown," I scream, grabbing the gun in a desperate attempt to stop him.

He pushes me away and wraps the other arm around the man's neck, applying more pressure. His face grows purple from lack of oxygen.

"He's no cop," he screams, ripping his arms apart in a sudden fit of rage and snapping the man's neck. The body falls at my feet, and he clamps a hand over my mouth. "Be quiet now, girl."

DREAMING OF VEGAS

I'm being kept a prisoner in this hotel room with Mr. Brown watching my every move. He does leave at times, but I've no idea what he does during his hours away. Is he with Ray? Do they talk about me? So many questions fly through my mind that I end up not able to concentrate on my writing.

It's odd to share a room with Mr. Brown. I want my own place, an apartment to call my own. I don't mind his presence, but I just hate being under his control and how he dismisses my wishes. His feelings for me become apparent when I parade around the room wearing nothing except a t-shirt. *Yeah, I can be naughty.*

Even now, he's watching me write. He sits in the armchair, pretending to read the morning paper. But I feel his glances at my body, which bring a smile to his lips. It makes me happy that his hungry eyes stare at me so often, looking as if he could grab me and possess me at any moment.

"Do you wish to read my new story?" I ask him.

No reply.

"I dreamed of you last night, girl," he says, eyes locking onto mine.

My words fail me as my chest constricts and the air is forced from my lungs. Shall I tell him that I dream of him as well? I wish to feel his strong hands upon me, bringing me into submission. Rip this shirt off me, ravish me, and do what you will, Mr. Brown.

"Yes?" I manage and wait for him to continue.

He rises from the chair and pours a large glass of wine, taking half of it down in one gulp. "Never mind, girl, I am not meant to speak to you in this way." He finishes the glass and pours more.

I close my eyes and listen to the air escaping his lips in a raspy whistle. "Oh, Mr. Brown," I sigh, turning on the television.

It is cold and windy today in Las Vegas, and I want to cuddle with Mr. Brown and watch movies. Too bad he isn't the cuddling type. He allows me to put my head on his shoulder and place my arm across his chest but no more. It vexes me. I feel a flush in my face as I write, knowing he's watching as I think about him. Can he read my thoughts? He must feel my need for him.

Pouring myself a glass of wine, I drink and drift into my mind. These days are filled with frustration. I wait for Ray, yearn for Mr. Brown, and sit in anticipation of summer. July feels like a year away.

***

How did this come to be, Mr. Brown? You're lying beside me shirtless, arms behind your head, and snoring. And I smile. I run a finger over the thick denim and tug at the button, but you don't even flinch.

I sit and grab my notebook off the table, and wait for my mind to focus on an idea. My leg keeps shaking, so I get up to change the temperature.

What am I to do with you? At first, I paraded around in skimpy clothing to tease you, and now you are the one half-naked while I'm wearing pajamas. I notice that you have lost your pants. You remain asleep. A part of you, anyway. I can't suppress a small giggle and hold the notebook in front of my face. I stop when I contemplate sleeping next to you.

Will he take me in my sleep? Will I protest or scream? I want him to tear my clothes and take me without a word. But that's for him to decide. Pulling off my pajamas in a rush, I dive under the covers naked and place my head against his shoulder. Sleep coming on as I fight to stay awake...

I feel hands upon me. He looks concerned. My arms flail to push him away as I try to lift myself. I'm drowning, so I grab him. I hit and scratch him. He envelops me in his arms and whispers in my ear.

"You had a nightmare," he says.

***

I can't piece together what happened last night or how I came to be nestled in his arms when I woke up this morning. Now, I sit in the recliner with my knees tucked to my chest and against my chin. The water from the shower drips onto my arms, and I make no attempt to get a towel. He's watching me with the usual desire absent. I avoid his attempt to make eye contact.

He grunts at me as he grabs the brush off the dresser. He gestures for me to get off the chair. I stand, watching him sit down before pulling me between his legs. The brush catches on snarls, and he presses his face into my curls.

"You smell like apricots," he whispers, brushing my hair once again.

I sit numb with his legs still wrapped around me, locking me inside a cocoon of warmth. Feeling his lips against my neck soft and light, I relax my shoulders and give in. The touch of his hands against my body brings heat to my face. He sways as he holds me, squeezing me with thick arms until I am swallowed in his embrace.

"Tell me about your dream, girl," he whisper again into my ear.

I feel a chill run over my body as hot breath touches my neck. His hand goes lower on my stomach, and I gasp when he grabs me there.

"No," I say, and he releases me for a moment.

I make no move to separate because the touch of his skin against mine calms my nerves. As if sensing my thoughts, he slides an arm across my chest and pulls me against him.

"Why can't you speak about it?" he asks, clutching me even tighter, his palm cupping my breast and squeezing.

"Because nobody would believe me if I told them the truth."

He wipes tears away from my cheek. I am too emotional to say anything more. Pushing us off the chair, he carries me to the bed and pull the sheets over my body before getting in next to me, once again wrapping his arms and legs around me. He kisses my neck and shoulders as the tears flow. I can do nothing to stop the storm, a deep sob escaping my lips. Tucking my face into his arm, I let myself drift into him as sleep descends over my thoughts.

***

I stare out the window as I wait for words and thoughts to resolve into sentences. The tourists pour out of the casino into the hot Vegas afternoon.

Spring vaults into early summer in a flash in this city. People are in shorts, tank tops, and flip-flops when a mere week ago, they were wearing hooded sweatshirts and jeans.

I'd rather sit by the pool or sip a margarita at the bar than wait for the muse to strike me with lightning. Being in this room alone for weeks are starting to affect me because I am certain I hear voices. And I don't mean the ones inside my head. The need to finish this novel exerts a physical pressure that I feel in my chest, a tightness that extends into my stomach that keeps me awake at night and staring at the ceiling.

When I flip through my notebook, a loose sheet of paper falls from the pages. It's an old letter from Ray. I know it by memory, and as I close my eyes, I can hear his voice reading the words to me.

...you are not ready for this, you have yet to live. What have you experienced? Don't come to me until you have done things, seen things. Finish the novel, drive across country, have a few affairs...live before you tell me I am the only one for you and that we are destined to be together.

I want to speak with him, so I can tell him about my adventures. I have driven across the country and slept with random men, enough to say I'm experienced. As for this novel, I shall finish it before our meeting. It's my motivation. I can't wait to see the look on his face when I place my finished manuscript in his hands.

My phone is buzzing, but I don't answer. I won't talk to him. Stuffing my writing supplies, I walk out of the room. There must be inspiration somewhere in this casino, right? I can't sit locked up in the room like a prisoner. I have to live. After all, I'm only following his words.

The casino is almost empty today with just a small group of tourists surrounding the pool entrance. I get in line without knowing it, standing behind a group of local college boys. One boy with blond hair, no shirt, and well-toned muscles glistening with bronzer eyes me and smiles. I decide to grab a chair near his group, following them at a close distance. They seems to be debating about which member of the group will get a girl first.

Taking my notebook from the backpack, I place it on my stomach but leave it closed. I'm sure that the blond boy will talk to me soon enough. To my surprise, he throws a towel onto the chair and jumps into the pool. Grabbing my pen, I open the notebook and write.

Men are stupid.

I hear laughter and turn to see an older gentleman in the chair next to me. He's peeking over my shoulder and reading what I wrote. Closing my notebook, I glare at him and wait for him to speak.

"You are quite right," he says, winking at me. His gaze follows my blond boy as he swims a few laps of the pool.

"Don't you know it's rude to spy on people?" I say, turning in the chair to face him.

He chuckles, and I smile in spite of my feigned anger because I'm loving his low, comforting voice. I kick off my flip-flops and cross my legs, giving him a generous view of thigh.

"You look like someone I know," I say to him as the blond boy flops on the chair next to me, splashing water on my notebook.

Turning to him, my first thought is that his eyes are a pretty shade of blue, and I forgive him getting water on my journal.

"You're hot," he says, rubbing a towel over his chest and giving me what I think he means to be a sexy smile.

"Tell me he didn't say that," I say, turning to the older man, but the chair next to me is empty.

"Who are you talking to?" he asks.

"I was talking to Ray," I answer after a short pause.

He stares at me for a long while, mouth widening.

I grab my notebook and write again.

She soon invites him back to her room to prevent him from speaking. He is beautiful, but she knows if she makes him think, his brain might explode. This is destined to be a physical relationship.

"Listen, you're in over your head here," I say.

"You don't know me. You don't even know my name."

"Yes, I do. You're called chapter ten, and I will tell you what your name is tonight. So, Brad, will you please take me up to my room and undress me?"

He walks behind her in silence, following her into the elevator. He doesn't touch her in any way before she leads him into the room by the towel around his neck. After closing the door, she pulls the towel off him and throws it onto the armchair with her backpack.

"My name is Eric," he says.

"Brad," I insist.

He begins to speak, but I hold up my hand for him to stop. I reach into my bag, pull out the room keycard, and place it into his hand.

"This isn't up for discussion," I say, standing and throwing the backpack over my shoulder. I walk some twenty paces toward the elevator before I look over my shoulder to see him less than an arm's length behind me. With a smile, I press the button for my floor as he stands close to me. Already, his hand is brushing against my thigh, and the tips of his fingers lingers on my skin.

"What is your name?" he asks as the elevator rises.

"That is none of your concern." The bell rings to signal my floor.

Do as you are told, and do not ask questions. You are in over your head. Pretend I'm the blonde girl from across the hall in your dorm. Got it? There is nothing else to see here. I'm a simple, garden variety slut. I am not secretly planning your demise with each thought in my mind. Never. I swear. Good night, sir.

FOR THE RECORD

Waking on an empty bed and the sun leaking through the blinds, I rub my temples and grab the water bottle. My head is pounding from hangover and dehydration. I really need to make a habit of consuming water when I drink alcohol. Maybe I need to put a voice reminder in my phone because I never want to feel this overwhelming nausea again anytime soon.

I can't recall the events of last night as I look around the room. I see nothing except empty wine bottles. Where did the boy go? Did he spend the night? These questions swim in my mind as I stagger to the bathroom and start the shower.

Leaning my head against the tile in this enormous shower, I let the water scald my skin. I try to collect the snapshots floating in my head into something resembling a coherent memory. I remember sending the boy for a bottle of whiskey, but after that, it is all a jumble of shots, flirting, and wrestling on the carpet. I let the boy pin me and grope to his heart's content, but I can't recall anything else.

Fighting the urge to fall asleep under the water, I manage to put conditioner in my hair and grab the razor to shave with special care. I step from the glass enclosure, wrap a towel about my shoulders, and walk into the bedroom. I pick an outfit from the clothes tossed onto the couch.

I'm holding a pleated, plaid skirt, Ray's favorite, when I hear grunting sounds coming from the second room. A small bit of memory from yesterday makes me smile. I enter the room with the towel draped across an arm but covering almost nothing. Mr. Brown is tied to a chair with his arms and legs bound by thick rope and a generous amount of duct tape covering his mouth.

His eyes narrow, and he moves his hands to rock the chair beneath him. I tied the knots myself, so I know he's not going to escape. He must be angry.

"Will you behave?" I laugh.

I hear more grunts and wait for him to be still before I peel the tape away from his lips. After, I put a finger on his lips and whisper into his ear not to speak. I retrieve the water bottle from the other room and hold it against his mouth, pouring a small amount for him to drink.

"What kind of stunt is this?" he says after he swallows the water. Some of it drips down his chin.

I wipe his face with the towel and run a hand through his hair. I straddle the chair and sit on his lap. "I will not be your prisoner, Mr. Brown," I whisper into his ear as I continue running my nails over his scalp.

"You are not a prisoner. You're free to do what you will as long as you stay away from certain people," he says, the anger still in his voice.

I caress his cheek. "Oh, Mr. Brown, you are in no position to tell me what to do."

He grinds his teeth. I laugh as he continues trying to pull his hands free from the rope.

"Can you at least put on clothes?" he asks, trying to avert his eyes from my skin.

Shaking my head, I laugh again. Adjusting on his lap, I press myself against him and grind on his jeans, which brings a groan from his lips.

"Ray gave you to me. I don't take orders from you. It's the opposite, I can assure you." Making a motion with my eyes over the ropes, I hope to impress upon him my meaning.

He grunts again and turns his eyes away from me. That doesn't stop me from wrapping my arms about his neck and pulling myself against his chest.

"No more boys in here. It isn't safe. Anyone can be a spy," he says.

I grab his face and make him look into my eyes. "Are you jealous?" I grin.

"I can't keep you safe tied to a chair," he growls, ignoring my question.

"You're not here to protect me. You're here to obey me," I scream into his ear and get off of his lap. I walk into the other room and put on shorts and a tank top before grabbing my knife off the table.

I see a smile on his face when he sees the knife. I pull a chair next to his and sit.

Laughing, I cross my legs. "Why is Ray making me wait?"

Nothing.

With a sigh, I free one of his hands and sit back. He flexes his hand and moves his fingers before attempting to pull at the knot restraining his other arm. I wave his hand away and cut through the other rope, freeing the second one. Rubbing at his wrists, he winces in pain.

"This is bigger than you can imagine."

With a laugh, I cut the rope from his ankles. He tries to stand but falls back onto the chair.

"Sit for a minute," I say, rubbing at the white rings around his wrist.

Lifting his arm, I kiss his skin, which feels abrasive against my lips. His hands grip my upper arms, and his fingers pinch my skin. I yelp in pain as he pulls me on his lap.

"No more boys," he demands.

"I promise, Mr. Brown," I answer as I feel his hands on me. "Now tell me what I want to know."

***

I take my time organizing everything on the tray. I want it to be perfect. Coffee with cream to the right of crispy bacon, and two eggs over medium served with the morning paper. Tying the robe about my waist, I push my feet into the new slippers and carry the tray into the sitting room to Mr. Brown. He pretends to be watching a news program on TV, but I see the corners of his mouth lift, a smile fighting though his efforts to appear serious.

"The morning paper." I place the tray on the beveled glass table in front of him. I run a finger over ice sculpture figurines etched into the glass as I wait for him to speak to me. The tightness spreads in my stomach.

He grabs the paper without a word and eases back on the leather couch, scanning the headlines before taking a sip of the coffee. "Less cream," he says.

Sudden heat in my face makes me want to snap at him, but I hold my tongue. He glances at me and pats a hand against his leg. Without a fight, I sit on his knee and let him wrap an arm around my back.

"You could read the news on my tablet," I say to him, moving closer to his body.

"I don't read on plastic." His voice is so low that it's closer to a growl, but again, a smile betrays him.

When I slap at the paper, he makes a show of being mad, but I kiss his neck several times. Placing the paper on the table, he turns and gets on top of me.

"Let me have my breakfast, girl," he groans, eyes scanning the folds of my robe.

"Yes, Mister Brown," I mumble, waiting to see where he will touch me.

Instead, he pulls away, eats a piece of bacon and washes it down with a mouthful of coffee. I smile and go fetch the pot in the kitchenette. He pushes the empty plate toward me as I fill his cup and nods toward the small pantry area.

"More, Mister Brown?" I smile.

He grunts his approval, and I set about making a second breakfast. While I'm frying the eggs, he turns on the financial.

"The Federal Reserve Bank is going to step in with more easing soon." His eyes narrow as he watches the scroll of endless letters and numbers at the bottom of the screen.

I serve him another plate and watch him make a few notes in ink in the newspaper margins. Trying to see what he's writing, I lean over him and place a hand on his leg to balance myself. He brushes my hand away, so I give up my attempt, leaning my head on his shoulder.

"Why is the Federal Reserve Bank important?"

"The Fed controls the money," he answers without pause, pulling my cheek against his chest.

Deciding to hold my comment for now, I watch the TV with him. I place my hand on his stomach and rub my nails over his white t-shirt as a pretty lady yawns on and on about the six month old bull market being 'tired.' As I do not know how long it takes bulls to get tired, how am I to know if this is good news or bad?

"What is a bull market?" I ask.

Jumping from the couch, he paces the room and grabs the coffee off the table. "What am I going to do with you? I'm trying to talk to you about something serious, and you're caught up with getting me..."

Stopping next to the table, he pauses and looks down at me, taking even breaths and flexing his fingers. "Stop pushing me every moment. Just stop." He places the cup on the table before thudding down next to me on the couch.

I remain still until his anger subsides. Slipping my hand into his, I turn my attention back to the TV show and make an effort to comprehend what I see. Seeing a pattern of letters in the constant crawl, I clear my throat to speak.

"The ones I see the most are the popular stocks?"

He squeezes my hand. I take the opportunity to lay my head on his arm, keeping my eyes on the television.

"Not always in a good way," he says with a chuckle.

As I look up at him, he takes my face in his hands and kisses me, slowly parting my lips and teasing me with his tongue. The moment passes as he pulls away, but the warmth remains.

"I'm a quick learner," I whisper as he kisses me again, this time with more force, pushing me against the couch.

I expect a response, but instead, his hands pull my robe apart, exposing my stomach and chest. He presses his beard into my neck as he kisses my ear, hands squeezing and pinching.

"Oh, Mr. Brown," I gasp.

***

Mr. Brown looks around for the waitress while both of us ignore my phone beeping at short intervals. My eyes stay on his face, not afraid to look at his scar. A short girl with shoulder-length brown hair arrives at the table, not the same girl who took our order.

"Two shots of whiskey," he says.

When she checks me out, Mr. Brown tells her that both shots are for him.

Leaning back against the booth, I study his face as the waitress places the shots on the table and hurries away. He pushes one toward me and grunts before taking his shot.

"Not tonight, Mister Brown," I say, smiling as he takes the other shot. "Enjoy yourself. I promise to watch you later."

"We shouldn't be here," he says in a low voice, looking around the room again.

"Relax. You're so paranoid. We walked through the casino. No harm in that, is there? Nobody saw us, I assure you."

"Do not speak..." he begins to answer, but the waitress is standing next to the table with the food.

The brunette places a tray on a stand and a plate in front of each of us. She doesn't ask if we need anything and leaves in a hurry, not making eye contact with Mr. Brown.

"I think you scare her." I wink before I cut into my prime rib. "Ooh, rare for once. The last time, I got a piece closer to medium."

He looks for the waitress again, and I know being in public with me is making him nervous. I can't understand what he can be afraid of...he's a mountain of a man at 6'6" and 280 pounds.

"Eat your dinner." I carve away the marbled fat and cut the meat into small pieces before I begin eating.

His scar is bright red and throbbing as his hand grips the knife.

I chew with care as he stares at me. "Do you need me to cut your meat? I'm pretty handy with a knife."

A chuckle escapes his lips, and his shoulders relax. I know he can't stay mad at me. Motioning to the waitress, he orders a bottle of wine. After the girl leaves it on the table, he pours a glass for me.

"You are pretty," he says, extending his glass in my direction.

"Thank you, Mister Brown." I touch glasses, smiling inside before taking a sip of Cabernet.

He empties the glass and pours another with his eyes still upon me, which are softer than usual.

"Why are you afraid to be here with me?"

He finishes the bottle of wine and calls for another. "If Ray saw us..."

"Don't worry about Ray." My phone buzzes yet again. I hold it up and turn it, so Mr. Brown can see Ray's name on the screen.

"I should not have given you his number," he says, gulping down more wine.

"He's texting me now, so I think we can say it is quite fine with him," I respond.

"What if he finds out about us?" His fist slams against the table, spilling some of my wine.

"He will find out if you keep acting like a fool," I say in as stern a voice as I can muster.

He grins at me.

Shaking my head, I signal to the waitress for the check. Mr. Brown stuffs a few hundred dollar bills into her hand, smiling as her jaw drops.

"Have the wine sent up to the room," he says to the waitress. "Make it a few bottles to be on the safe side."

***

I grab ice cream from the freezer and curl up in the recliner. Mr. Brown tears through wine, the sign of a nasty drunk emerging. When he puts an action movie on TV, I offer no commentary. Instead of watching the movie, he stares at me with hints of red coloring the whites of his eyes. He taps a hand on the couch next to him, and the other hand holds the wine bottle.

Taking a last bite before returning the ice cream to the kitchenette, I sit next to him. I grab his hand and put it on my leg before taking the remote from him and changing the channel. He grips my thigh and squeezes, fingers turning white as he digs into my skin.

"Everything is a manipulation," he slurs, eyes seeing the fantasy show on the television.

"Are you going to complain all night because I mentioned Ray? Grow up." I reach for his hand, but he flails his arm to break free and pulls at my pajamas. "Stop it."

Pushing me against the arm of the couch, he climbs on me, breathing hot wine against my neck. "You think you can play me?" he growls at me, pushing a hand under my chin and gripping my throat.

I fall limp into his hands without resistance. Fingers wrap around my windpipe. I close my eyes, hoping he'll be quick about whatever he's planning. I hear my phone ring, and my eyes snap open. He instantly lets me go.

Diving toward the table, I grab my phone and press the button.

"Ella?" I hear a deep bass voice I think is Ray and it brings a smile to my face.

"Ray!" I yell into the phone.

"Give me that." Mr. Brown tries to take the phone.

I push at him, but he falls on top of me, crushing me against the couch. Clutching the phone in my hand, I curl into a ball, trying to keep it away from him.

"Ray, where are you?" I scream into my hand, but before I hear a response, Mr. Brown rips the phone from me and ends the call.

I feel him pulling at my pajamas again, but I don't put up a fight. There is no point in fighting him. One hand yanks my hair as he presses against me, and the other is punctuating the assault with a hard slap against my bare ass.

"Stop, please," I say.

"I want you to want this," he slurs into my ear.

Moving my legs apart, I look into his glassy eyes. "I do, sir, I do," I say, putting my arms around his neck and closing my eyes.

I'm coming, Ray. Very soon. Everyone tries to keep me away from you, but it will not deter me. I shall look upon your face within the week, if the gods be good. Until then my love, adieu.

AT THE GYM

I feel the rhythm of my strides in the music, a dance number that propels me to increase the tempo on the treadmill. Thoughts of last evening cloud my mind as I fight to keep pace with the machine, and my breathing gets more difficult as the song changes in my headphones. Mr. Brown scares me when he drinks. He becomes more violent with each passing hour, with each sip he takes. His desire for me had no bounds, and he went on for most of the night. When I woke up this morning, I was relieved to see him still asleep.

Now, I don't know what to think. All I know is that I miss him and wish he were here. I feel a conflict in my stomach as I ponder leaving him in a few days to find Ray. Why do things have to change? Can't he stay my Mr. Brown? Am I being greedy? I increase the pace and try to push the thoughts out of my mind as my heartbeat becomes a part of the music. His words echo, and I push myself harder. My legs burns from the increasing resistance of the machine.

What if he finds out about us?

No answers rise to his eternal question. I tap on the buttons to raise the incline to the steepest angle I have yet to achieve. With one last burst of manic energy, I push for a full minute on this new settling before my body screams for mercy and I begin to lower the incline. As my breathing regulates and my legs shake with effort, I hear his voice from somewhere near me.

I find him in the hallway, talking on his phone near the gym entrance. My heart skips a beat, and I almost fall off the machine. He smiles as he sees me and I smile in return, wondering if he will take me to lunch after I shower. Grabbing a towel from my bag, I wipe the sweat. I yelp with surprise when he grabs my wrist with his hand.

"Where have you been?" he growls, his grip hurting my arm. I have time to stuff my phone and towel into my bag before he pulls me toward the entrance.

"Stop, you're hurting me," I say as the attendant at the desk yells for me to wait.

"Don't forget your bags, miss," the young woman says, handing me three bags with different store labels.

Mr. Brown takes the bags and leaves the gym without another word. I follow him at a short distance, hoping he'll calm down. When the elevator door closes, he drops the bags and puts his hands on my shoulder. I wonder if he's going to hit me or kiss me. Instead, he pulls my face against his chest and kisses the top of my head.

"You weren't in the room when I woke up. I thought you left me and didn't say goodbye."

I fight the urge to laugh, knowing it will make him angrier. His hands clench around my shoulders, and I wait until he swipes the keycard to open the room.

"After staying with me for over a month, you should know that I'll tell you when I'm going to leave. I won't sneak away in the night."

I walk to the bathroom and begin shedding my gym clothes to shower. He sits on the toilet, just watching me.

"Can I have a few minutes to myself, please?" I close the glass shower door behind me and get under the water. I can see him going through my shopping bags through the glass door.

"These shops aren't in this casino. You agreed to stay here."

Raising my middle finger, I yell, "I did not agree to that, and you know it."

He takes out my new pink shorts and holds them up, examining and giving a small laugh. I smack my hand on the glass.

"If you're going to annoy me, at least get in here and wash my back," I say, holding out the facecloth.

"Yes, master." He winks and enters.

I look down, and this time, I just can't stop from laughing. "Keep that thing away from me, Mister!"

I turn, so he can wash my back. His hand slides down my arm, and I lean my cheek against the glass. He rubs the cloth on my skin in slow circles, caressing and kissing me. Working down my legs, he rubs with both hands, massaging tired muscles.

"I'm sorry for grabbing you earlier."

"Why can't you enjoy our time together without getting crazy about what may or may not happen in the future?"

Instead of words, he stands and wraps his arms around my waist, turning me toward him. He holds me in his arms, cradling my face in his hands. Water drips off his face onto my body. Pushing me against the glass, he kisses my neck and shoulders, his beard tickling my skin. As he rubs a finger against my cheek, he pulls away from me.

"I'll see about lunch." He kisses me before leaving.

Oh, Mr. Brown, listen to what a woman means and not what she says.

***

While I brush my hair, I hear the first notes of a piano on the stereo. Putting on a robe, I walk into living room. Mr. Brown is gone. My writing desk is set for work with my notebook next to the tablet along with a steaming cup of coffee. Walking to the entertainment center, I can see the details of the music playing, Miles Davis, "Kind of Blue," a favorite of mine while I write. Smiling at his thoughtful pick, I sit at the desk and take up my pen.

He seems to be able to read my mind and soul at times. Can he not know what...?

I stop, deciding to keep the thought to myself. He may read this journal. One can never be too sure. As a trumpet and sax dance to a slow snare beat, I click on my novel and read a few paragraphs as the music mixes with my words.

Mr. Brown enters and places a box of pizza on the kitchenette counter before sitting in the armchair nearest to me. Using the remote to increase the volume, he taps his foot along with the beat, watching me read. Holding the tablet in my hands, I turn the chair to face him and put my feet on his lap. He shakes a finger at me, but as always, he smiles in spite of any show of anger.

"Why aren't you writing?"

Looking up at him, I laugh, which leads to a deep blush spreading over my face. "I have my ending, Mr. Brown." I wink.

"Is that a fact?" He glares at me, and the thin smile leaves his face. "I hate that you call me Mr. Brown."

Putting my feet on the floor and the tablet on my lap, I take my coffee in my hands and lean against the desk.

"You gave me no other name, so I can't do anything about that particular complaint." I return my gaze back to my tablet.

He can be such a woman sometimes.

"That doesn't keep it from annoying me."

"Can we not do this today? It's beautiful outside, and I was hoping to get some sun after I finish reading over my last few chapters."

His growl only tells me that he won't take me outside unless he drinks a few glasses of wine. You can't get that man in a bathing suit when he's sober. Forget it. Shutting down the tablet so he can't snoop, I walk into the kitchenette and open a bottle of wine.

Grabbing my purse from the counter, I turn to make sure he's not behind me. I find a prescription bottle and remove two bar-shaped pills. I crush them and put the powder into Mr. Brown's wine, mixing it in with my fingers. Putting the bottle into my bag, I take the glasses into the other room as the music changes to a hard rock number that isn't on my writing playlist.

"Why did you change the music?" I hold out a glass of wine to him.

"You are not writing, so I'll listen to what pleases me." He eyes the wine but leaves his hands on his lap. "Wine at noon?"

"I am going tanning, and I know you need wine for that to happen, so drink up," I say.

He drains the glass in one motion and slams the glass on the table, cracking the base. Reaching for mine, he takes it and drinks before throwing the glass into the fireplace against the wall.

"I'm tired of taking orders from you," he growls, wine dripping over his beard.

I return to the kitchen and pour another glass, sipping it as I join him again. "Are you done with your tantrum?"

Instead of answering, his eyes are on my wine. With a sigh, I walk to his side and hold the wine out of his reach. "Behave," I say, taking another sip of wine before handing him the glass.

He makes a motion of taking a small drink and pats a hand on his leg.

"No, I'll sit at the desk."

With a grunt and a slight rise of his shoulders, he drinks wine before using the button to lift the footstool. He thuds each foot onto the rest and smiles at me through the wine glass.

"Are you trying to get me drunk to take you to the pool or some other reason?" he asks, his voice cracking.

Can the pills be working on him already?

"To make you be nice," I answer, parrying his attempt to start an argument.

"No, no, you're up to something. You haven't asked me where Ray is for days." He taps a finger against the glass.

197

"I stopped wasting my time. You won't talk. Voluntarily." Walking into the bedroom, I remove my robe.

He follows me, but I don't face him. Putting on my bathing suit, I lift my hair and wait for him to get the hint to take the strings I am holding. I feel his hands at my neck, and he takes some time touching my skin before tying a knot.

"You don't want to know." He kisses me below the ear.

"On that point you are incorrect," I say without hesitation.

His jaw drops, he paws at his face, and I giggle as he sits on the bed. "I don't understand."

Pulling a tank top over my head to go with light blue shorts, I pause before answering. "I told you I needed to finish my novel. This is about more than Ray."

He places a hand against his forehead, and his head pitches forward. "I feel lightheaded."

Pushing my hand into his chest, I lay him on the pillows and pull off his shoes.

"I have one question," I say, turning on the television and putting on the baseball game that always plays in Ray's library at Holden Farms.

"What's that?"

I can't imagine what's flying through his mind right now under the influence of a bottle of wine and a two days' worth of happy pills.

"What's the significance of the baseball game?"

His eyes close for a moment, but I pinch his arm to wake him. "There is none," he slurs before closing his eyes again.

***

Bottles of chilled wine and a fruit tray crowd the bedside table while I wait for him to wake up. My eyes run over rope and naked flesh. I'm quite sure I see his eyes flutter a little as I pour myself a glass. Consciousness mixes with understanding as he tests the restraints, pulling with sudden strength. He soon stops the struggle and watches as I grab a handful of fruit. Eating and sipping wine, I smile at him.

"This doesn't fit your pattern," he says, voice cracking with the effort of speaking.

I snort and spit wine on him. I need a few moments to stop coughing before I can speak. "Pattern?" I mimic, laughing and chewing a strawberry.

"Yes, it is a change from your routine. Don't be coy with me."

"I have killed three men, so how can there be a pattern?" I ask as I tilt my head and smile at him again.

Staring at me for a moment, his mouth moves several times without a sound escaping his lips.

"Ten," he says.

Ten? There is no way it is possible.

"Three," I say again, grabbing the knife from the tray and wiping the blade free of juice and pulp.

"Ten," he repeats, glaring at me.

With a laugh, I press the blade against his neck, which makes him pull against the ropes. I run the blade along his skin, making a pencil thin blood line under his beard.

"How about we make it eleven?" I ask him, stopping for a moment to take a sip of wine.

He thrashes at his restraints again, shaking the bed in his fury. I laugh at his rage and put the wine on the table. Clapping at his effort, I blow a kiss to him before I again take up the knife.

"If you kill me, you'll never know," he says, spitting at me.

"Oh?" I take a seat on the bed next to him. I smile and wait for him to continue. Nothing he can say will hurt me. "Well, get on with it. Tell me the truth."

"You're being lied to for the money. It's all a charade."

"I don't know what you're hinting at. Speak, so I can understand. And don't think for a moment any information you give will save you. Ray told me that you were the one he hired to kill my father. You were the one that failed."

"I don't deny it. He paid me, and I didn't finish the job. That doesn't change the fact that what I'm telling you is true. The man you knew died."

"I don't understand."

"Ray killed himself."

The room spins, and I grip my fingers in his beard to keep from falling. What he says can't be true, but the words cut into my stomach like fact.

"You lie," I whisper.

Silence ticks. His breathing slows, and I listen and wait.

"He died in a terrorist attack. One of his own planning. Textbook suicide."

I stagger away from the bed, lurching toward the window facing Las Vegas Boulevard. Tears in my eyes turn the lights into a blur of runny neon. I pound my fists against the glass.

"It can't be true. I saw him on the television."

"The man you knew as a child is dead, I say," he spits at me. "The person answering your texts is Ryan. His brother. Ray is dead. Get it through your skull."

"No, you are wrong. It can't be Ryan. I saw him on television with a woman. I'm not crazy. I saw a woman."

He coughs and wheezes before speaking. "Woman?"

"His wife."

I hear him laughing and pivot toward him.

"The wife died many years ago. I don't know if you're crazy, but you didn't see him on television," he says.

Walking to the bed, I extend my arm and place the knife against his neck. It is pointless to argue with this man. I'm done with his lies. Leaning closer, I ask, "Why didn't you kill my father? Ray paid you. Why didn't you do it?"

"I investigated..." he starts before pausing. Can he say it? "I saw with my own eyes what Ray did to you. It seemed to me he wanted your father dead to cover..."

"Say it, and you die."

"Ray molested you. And that's why I didn't kill your father."

The words scrape the insides of my brain and cause a physical pain inside my skull. I can feel the scream building in my stomach and grip a handful of his hair, pulling and thrashing at him.

"He didn't molest me," I scream, my arms moving, the blade making cuts in his face and neck. "Take it back. You take it back, right now. Take it back."

I scream and wail, thrashing my arms until I can't see or hear or feel anything. Stopping, I see the bed awash in blood and the thing that was Mr. Brown an unrecognizable pulp of seeping wounds.

Staggering and slipping my way to the window, I put my hands on the glass and look down upon the tourists, blood dripping down the pane from my fingers. My head swims, and I fight to steady my vision. Slowly, I see the city through the glass.

"Hello, Las Vegas."

ABOUT THE AUTHOR

Stephen John Moran lives in Vegas with his beautiful wife Maggie, two dogs and a cat. He is the author of many novels and short stories, with Ella being the first publication. Stephen enjoys reading, sports, and spending time with his family.

Follow the Characters on Twitter –
@EllaThomas22 and @GeorgeinVegas
Read Ella's Journal at
http://www.stephenjohnmoran.com/ellas-journal
Follow the story at
http://www.stephenjohnmoran.com/
For information contact
StephenJohnMoran@gmail.com